LIZARDS, LOST FAIRIES

short stories by
Bettianne Shoney Sien

Acknowledgements:
I would like to thank Irene Reti, owner of HerBooks, for her enthusiastic response to "Ida" back in 1985, which encouraged me to bring my work out of hiding, and for her commitment to lesbian-feminist writing.

Koré Hayes Archer has been an imaginative and supportive best friend for many years. Her writing and her always creative lifestyle have inspired me. Her care and feeding of this manuscript in each stage of its development have been crucial, as have our frequent discussions and rare hikes.

I wish to express my gratitude for the generous amount of time my good friend/lover De Clarke has given to almost every phase of this project, from graphic design to copy editing. I appreciate her ruthless intelligence, her *real* feminism, her writing, her music, and the good sense with which she usually leaves me alone.

Lizards/Los Padres. Copyright ©1988 by Bettianne Shoney Sien. All rights reserved.

Cover and inside illustration by Kendall Morris.

Publisher's Note:
These stories are works of fiction. Names, characters, places and incidents are either the product of the author's imagination or are used fictiously. Any resemblance to actual events or locales or persons, living or dead, is entirely coincidental.

"Ida" was published in *MAIZE* (Fall 1988) and in *Lesbian Words II: Photographs and Writings*. "My Mother Played the Accordion" appeared in *Sinister Wisdom* #36. "Marsha: 1962" (an earlier version of "Marsha: 1962" part 1) appeared in *The World Between Women: an Anthology*. "Lizards/Los Padres" appeared in *Common Lives/Lesbian Lives* #27.

This book may not be reproduced in whole or in part, except for purposes of reviews, without permission from HerBooks, P.O. Box 7467, CA 95061.

Printed in the United States of America by McNaughton & Gunn.

ISBN: 0-939821-32-X

CONTENTS

Ida	1
Prom	5
Sapphire Mountains	16
Crocks of Kraut	21
Killing Mice	33
Marsha: 1962	43
The Mouse-Gray Suitcase	73
Glad to Meet You	77
The Big Blue Ford	85
My Mother Played the Accordion	91
Wishing on White Horses	97
Cecropia Moths	114
Lizards/Los Padres	115

Ida

First thing I remember about Ida, she comes to the farm saying, "Got any of those big boys of yours around here to help me with my haying this year?"

My mom tells her no, they're all hired out to neighboring farms already. Nothing she can do to help her out.

Well, Ida's pretty desperate. She looks around, sees me. "What about that scrawny one?"

My mom snorts, says, "That girl's so lazy. You're not gonna get any kind of work out of her."

Ida says, "I'll give her a try, if you don't mind."

Mom looks at me, I don't say a word.

"You can take her."

Off I go.

"You drive a tractor?"

"Yeah."

Before I know it, I'm driving that baler, she's throwing bales of hay onto the wagon as fast as any man I ever saw, and she isn't that big either.

Curly hair, sunburnt face. She blows her nose on one of those big red handkerchiefs like any guy out there with all that dust blowing around.

She grabs a bale of hay, yells up at me: "Hey, look at this!"

I stop, get down. My legs are shaking from exhaustion, my nose must be as red as the barn.

What does she show me? A big rattlesnake wrapped right up into the bale of hay. She says, "Happens every year couple times. Never saw one this size before."

I get back on the tractor, back to work. We must have been out there six hours, never stopping except for a

Ida

few minutes after each load finishes going up the elevator into the haybarn.

Finally she says, "You're a real good worker. Scrawny though, how old are you? Ten? Eleven?"

"Almost thirteen."

"Twelve, then," she says. "Well, you're one good worker. I don't care what that mom of yours says."

After a while Ida says, "It must be three o'clock, pretty hot out here. Better stop, have a bite."

I say sure.

We go walking up the road to the farmhouse, kittens all over the place. One skinny old dog: Elmer, must be twenty years old, just panting in the shade.

There's Ida's mom: Pearl, she's almost eighty herself. Pearl says, "Who you got there?" Sets some apple pie, lemonade, in front of me.

Ida points at me, says, "This here is Bernice Greuning's girl."

"Never knew she had a girl."

"Only one, a darn good worker too," says Ida.

Well, I helped Ida out the rest of the summer. She gave me fifty dollars, told me she wanted me back again next year.

I heard her say to my mom, "Bernice, you can be real proud of this one."

My mom laughed like it was a joke.

In the fall I began high school. I was having a pretty hard time with my folks.

"All those boys," my mom would say to whoever would listen, "nine sons, and it's this girl who's gonna be the end of me."

They didn't like me wearing blue jeans all the time. I refused to go to church. My grades got worse.

Some teacher said to the high school counselor, "That girl shouldn't be going around all bruised up."

The counselor said to me, "I really suggest you find yourself a home where you can live in, work for room and board. Take care of kids or something. I don't think your parents will oppose the idea."

Right then and there I knew where I'd go, if she'd have me. Pearl had had a bad stroke in September, and I knew there was Ida having to take care of the farm and her mom all by herself.

The counselor drove me over to Ida's farm. We all sat and talked for a long while.

Finally, Ida leaned over to me, she said, "Listen, Hon, you think you can do it?"

She meant Pearl's chores: cooking dinners, caring for the garden, tending the chickens.

"I'd want you to help me with Pearl, too."

I nodded shyly, yes.

We shook hands. I moved in.

Well, I was pretty wound up in the beginning. Ida's house was so clean. Quiet, too. No brothers around to watch out for, no one sneaking into my room pestering me nighttimes. No one telling me what to do all the time.

I pitched right in. Started taking my workboots off before I came into the house, started looking out how I dressed (clean jeans).

I liked cooking for Ida 'cause she always said how good the food was. I followed Pearl's recipes, all neatly printed and filed in a little painted wooden box. We had chicken a lot; though I didn't like butchering, it had to be done. I feathered and gutted them, loving the silence of a quiet, clean house.

After dinner the cows had to be milked, then we'd come in and sit around the living room. I'd tell her about school, which I still hated; but I was getting better grades now.

She'd talk about her family, sadly about Pearl, who never spoke or recognized Ida again till the day she died three years later.

One time Ida showed me pictures of her and her friends from the army.

"Never heard of women in the army," I said.

Ida

"World War II," she replied; "my three brothers all went, only one came back. Pearl was terrified when I joined, but I was very patriotic," she raised an eyebrow, "at the time. Oh, they took whatever help they could get."

I told her how badly I wanted to have a different kind of life than I could have in our little town. I didn't know what.

"Yes," she told me, "you're a thinker, you wouldn't be happy doing this. And I don't think you're going to be lucky as I've been with this farm. Having all those brothers."

"So, you think maybe I should join the army?" I asked, but it sounded pretty awful to me, all those men bossing me.

"Good God, kid, you'd end up going crazy! I'd never join today. No, I think you'd better go to college."

Me, college? I'd never thought of that. No one I knew went to college. From then I thought of it a lot.

Once a week, she'd come in from the milking, get in the bathtub and soak for an hour, come out all fresh, a little *Evening in Paris* behind each ear, wearing some kind of pantsuit mail-ordered from Sears.

"You watch Pearl for me? You know where to get me if anything comes up."

Off she'd go to play cards until late into the night, a nickel a game, with Agnes and Minnie just as she had every Thursday night for the last twenty-five years.

"What do you all play?" I teased one night, "Old Maid?"

Well, it cracked her up!

She said with a wink: "A happier old maid you'll never find!"

Prom

"I can't believe you're not going to the wedding!" Vivian was carrying on, drink in one manicured hand, the other waving. "What *is* this? What are people going to *think*? And you moping around here for weeks. You should be standing there right by her side: maid of honor! You *know* her parents sent us invitations, what are we supposed to do?

"Of course, no one dreamed that I didn't already know! This is vulgar behavior, Linda, can't you patch up your petty little differences? My God, when will you grow up! You're always going to hate yourself for this. A girl only gets married once, and then they'll be all the way out in California. I am so embarrassed, I swear you're doing this just to humiliate me."

Linda continued chopping the chicken for the gourmet dish her mother was preparing; when she finished she began on the baby onions, letting her tears flow only a second before she swabbed them angrily away with her sleeve.

Linda thought of the fine white wine chilling and wished she could sneak the whole bottle into her room, forget glasses, be alone finally. She thought of the crisp green salad she had carefully arranged earlier, how she'd enjoyed balancing the ripe red tomato slices and brilliant baby carrots against the mix of subtle greens; it all seemed so alive. She thought of her grandmother who had taught her to cook, and sharply missed the woman who now lay in a nursing home unable to speak or to walk. She made herself think of anything but Sandy, and what her mother was saying. *Just let Mother wear herself out. Don't get caught in any of her traps.*

Linda refilled her mother's wineglass.

"What is your father going to say?" her mother asked, tapping her fingernails against the crystal.

Prom

When does he ever say anything? Linda knew that if she could keep her mouth shut, her mother would find some reason to dislike Sandy and defend her daughter, and she would let those reasons be known to all whose opinions counted so dearly. What reasons her mother invented, Linda didn't care; Sandy would be dead to them. Fine. That was the punishment Sandy deserved.

"Do you need me for anything else?" Linda kept her voice even as she washed her hands.

Her mother was absorbed in forming the pasta into elaborate shapes: meticulous, perfect shapes. It made Linda wish she would want to eat again someday.

Dismissed, Linda went to her old room and put on her sweatsuit. The several blocks to the lake she jogged. Stretching out on the strip along the water, she planned how far she would run today, farther than ever before.

"Liking high school is a symptom of some kind of disease," Caroline said as she looked through Linda's yearbook.

"Hey, girls' sports were in their infancy then. I played or wanted to play them all. You're just too stuck in your head. Best thing of all, I was good at them!" Linda flipped through the yearbook pages, then pointed at her picture. "See, I was voted Best Female Athlete senior year." She turned another couple of pages. "Class treasurer too."

"Yeah, but they would have tarred and feathered you if they knew you were a queer!"

Linda winced: *do you have to use that word?* Then she brightened: "But they didn't know, they'd never dream it in a million years."

"Well, doesn't it bother you? The lie?"

"It's not a lie. In some ways it makes it even better. I had one over on them the whole time." Linda laughed.

Swallowing her discomfort, Caroline pointed to the loose photo of Linda and Sandy, tucked into the album.

"Didn't you feel bizarre going to prom like that?"

"It was weird, I'll admit. But in the end it all worked out in my favor."

"Not in the very end." Caroline reminded softly.
"Yes, it did." Linda took her lover's hand.

"It was our senior year and Sandy let me know she had been asked to the prom. 'My whole family, they expect it. I can't let them down,' she said to me. See, she was the only girl in her family, so she had to do all the girl-things."

"Knowing how jealous you are, I'm surprised you didn't tell her right out that you didn't want her to go." Caroline said.

Linda took a hard look at Caroline, and understood in that moment why her lover would never make it in the corporate world.

"Are you serious? *Admit* I was jealous?"

"The thing is," Linda remembered, "I think Sandy got into it, she liked wearing the long gown. The whole trip."

Linda paused, then said, "No, there was only one thing to be done. Fight fire with fire."

"Boy, you spend so much time with each other, maybe the two of you should go to prom together instead!" David taunted Linda in the cafeteria. He wished she would take the hint and leave Sandy and him alone to eat lunch together.

Some of the guys from the team at the next table were signaling to him; he grinned and waved back. They had wanted to bet he couldn't score with Linda, but he hadn't taken them up on it. Not that he didn't like a challenge, but Linda? Well, she was popular and better looking than Sandy, he hated to admit, but Christ he wasn't going spend his allowance for nothing.

"Maybe we should," Linda dared him. "A double date would be a blast."

"Well, I ah, I guess," David fumbled. *Shit.* "It would depend a lot on who you're going with. I mean, who asked you out?"

"I don't want to say yet because I haven't given him my answer. See, the thing is, he's a nice guy, but not

Prom

really my type. If somebody I like better were to ask, then I could let this guy down easy: 'it was a hard choice.' You know, not hurt his feelings. I'd like to go with someone who's sweet, but not a wimp." Linda smiled at David. It reminded her of fishing out on Dad's CrisCraft.

David knew he had to think quick. *Len would be perfect. We've been buddies since sixth grade. Shit, he'd be cool on a double, we could plan it all out ahead of time. Yeah and if he got anything out of Linda, I'd be the first to know.*

"Say, Sandy, you think Linda would go with Len to the prom? He really wants to ask her," David asked after Linda finally left for Physics.

"What?" She gulped. "Gee, I didn't think Linda was interested in the prom," she replied, quickly grabbing her books to go. "Sure, ah, I guess she might."

"Let me tell you, it just thrilled Sandy's parents. The whole plan: the double date, me spending the night, since we were sure to get in late. Oh, they treasured the picture of David and Sandy ready to go out the door, but listen, they loved this one too."

Caroline looked closely at the loose photo she held: two teenage girls grinning, arm-in-arm, dressed in similar prom attire.

"I don't think I like this story."

"Just listen to the rest," Linda insisted, removing the photo from Caroline's critical eyes.

"You're a real doll!" Her mother's voice was high with excitement and liquor.

"Look, Henry, isn't she a doll?"

While her mother snapped pictures, her father shyly nodded.

"My best fishing buddy in a prom dress." He gave her a sympathetic wink.

Linda simmered. There had been no way to stop her mother from dragging her through this. Buying the dress had only been the first step in the nightmare, with Linda finally screeching at her mother right in the boutique:

"All right Mother, just pick it out yourself then. I don't care.'"

Vivian had scolded Linda, but gone ahead and done just that. She chose a baby pink satin empire gown that flowed out from under the breasts. There was an incredibly uncomfortable bra that Vivian insisted had to be worn with this type of dress. The sleeves of the garment gathered in tight elastic right at the bulk of Linda's arm muscle, and puffed out in what her mother called *Camelot Style.*

"It really is the perfect thing for your skin tone!" Linda's mother had exulted on the way home, oblivious to her sulking daughter.

"Linda, that's disgusting. How could you go through with it, why didn't you call it off?"

"It got out of hand. I didn't plan to tell my mother at all that I was going. I mean, I'm not sure what I thought I was going to do about the dress and all that stuff."

"You thought you could sneak to prom?"

"Well, like I said, I didn't have the whole game plan figured out. My damn boy-crazy sister heard at school. When Mom wouldn't give *her* permission to go, she got so pissed off she spilled the beans."

"Then how come *Linda* gets to go?" Mary burst out.

"For goodness sake, Mary, Linda is a senior. You can go next year."

Then Linda's mother turned and bore down on her. "My God, *why* don't you *ever* tell us anything? What's the idea? Do you think you can get any kind of dress at the last minute! I have to get you an appointment for your hair . . .*why* do you always do this to us? Who in the world asked you to go anyway?"

Under the rage, Vivian was thrilled.

"And I thought *my* parents were abusive," Caroline remarked.

"I made a silent pact to kill my little sister. What a

big mouth."

"I'm going with Leonard Burgess. The prom is two weeks away Mother, I was *not* waiting until the last minute."
"You don't know anything. Leonard who? Burgess?" Vivian knew fully well who Len was, she just had to pretend to evaluate his credentials. They more than measured up. *Knock it off mother. It's not like I'm going to marry the guy, no matter what you might wish.*
"Ohhhhhhhh, Leonard *Burgess.* Isn't that nice! I'm surprised his mother didn't call me to say something."
"I'm not going with his *mother,*" Linda said spitefully.

The school had hired a nice easy-rock band; David and Sandy, Len and Linda, danced to the pathetic suburban strains. Linda struggled to keep the bra-contraption from sliding down, to keep a smile on her face and her date on the right track.
Later, parked by Lake Michigan in David's father's Cadillac, the four drank brandy mixed into cans of Coke. Linda kept her eyes glued on Sandy, praying that David wouldn't lay a hand on her friend. She was certain she would punch him out if he did.
Eventually David suggested that he and Sandy go for a stroll along the lake. Antsy with Sandy out of sight, and having clearly shown a disinterest in kissing, Linda began a long distracted conversation about the track team. They made vague plans to do some running over the summer, and talked about college.
"Look, I think we'd better go find them."
"Uh, maybe they'd rather be left alone." Len went red. David would kill him if they interrupted the Big Plan.
"Well, I'm going!" Linda declared, and whipped off her high heels. She moved quickly out across the sand in her stocking feet.
Len came running after her; David could just think that they had accidentally stumbled onto them on their own walk. *Damn that jerk, he's probably out there get-*

ting some right now. I'm going to have to invent something good to beat him.

"Did you let him kiss you?"
It was six o'clock in the morning. Fifteen minutes earlier the girls had arrived at Sandy's house. They were now getting rid of their costumes.

Sandy's parents had got up in robes and slippers to greet the two. They didn't mind the late hour, they claimed. After all, as Sandy's dad put it: "I knew my little girl was in good hands with you, Linda."

Now, standing in Sandy's room, Linda posed the question again: "Well, did he kiss you?"

Sandy wondered how she was supposed to have stopped David without hurting his feelings. He had bought the tickets, the corsage, and dinner before the dance. How could she say no? *So I was a little bit curious. Linda's the only one who's ever kissed me. Does that even count? And anyway I always pretended that she's the man who'll marry me, after I go to med school and everything. I don't want to look dumb, it's practice. Of course, I can't tell Linda that. Well the thing is when Linda kisses me, it starts to feel so good that sometimes I forget to think about him . . .*

So naturally when David wanted to kiss me and I couldn't figure out how to say no, I figured well, why not check it out, kind of scientifically. Wouldn't it have to be better since it was the real thing? Even better than Linda's gentle mouth.

"This is getting more depressing by the minute. Predictable, too," Caroline interrupted. "Anyhow, how do you know she was thinking all that?"

"Hey, this is my life, okay. I know."

It was weird not to pull back from David's kiss, against instinct it seemed, to let him do it. The first kiss was very light, his test kiss: the one he used to show he was a gentleman, and to check out whether or not he was

11

going to encounter resistance. His kiss was warm and smelled like brandy; it wasn't *horrible*, but more than anything right then Sandy felt exhausted. She let herself sink back against his tuxedo; she let him hold her in his arms, hoping it would be restful like it was when Linda held her.

He understood her actions to mean: all systems go.

He started off slowly, then abruptly pushed his tongue into her mouth and ran his hand across the front of her dress. Sandy promptly gagged.

"HEY!" Disgusted, she pushed away from him.

Abruptly regaining herself, she rose, and began to brush the sand off her formal.

She politely smiled from her new height for a moment so he wouldn't think her rude, and then, surprised, pointed out over the lake: "David, look, the light!"

He stood and joined her to gaze at the lavender streaks forming across the horizon.

"Um, Linda, surely that's poetic license."
"I swear, it was. I saw it myself," Linda insisted.

"I've got to get back or my dad will be worried. You'll be in the doghouse, our dads won't be able to play golf together any more if you bring me home much later. Think what that will do to their scores."

Sandy began to walk in the direction of the car; it was then she saw the figure moving rapidly towards them. The pink gown was hiked up around the approaching figure's knees and the stride was clearly that of a track star.

Linda could see as she pulled off the pale dress that it was ruined: sweat stains under the arms, the hemline torn, water-stained. She didn't care. Her mother would be pissed off, but Linda had done this all for them anyhow. She had no intention of ever wearing the thing again regardless. She put on a teeshirt and crawled into Sandy's bed. Sandy was setting her glasses on the night stand. They pulled down the shade, and taped it against the window to make the room dark as possible.

"Well, didn't you kiss *Len*?" Sandy asked weakly.

"Did you like kissing a boy? Was it *nice*?" Linda cut through the diversion with what she hoped sounded like curiosity, not bitterness.

"Don't cry, Caroline."

"I will if I have to. It's enough to make a dyke hate straight women. It's the betrayal. It still hurts even at our age. You still say you loved high school?"

"Your problem is you think about everything too much," Linda replied. "It turned out to be a good night after all."

Sandy didn't want to talk about the stupid kiss any more. Exhausted, she hoped they could just sleep, but she couldn't stop thinking *I don't get it. I like Linda better. I can't, it's too weird.*

The blanket and pillow got shuffled around again; Sandy told her head to shut up.

I want her to kiss me.

Only to erase that gross slobbering.

If I promise it really is just practice, if I make my mind stay on that, then it's no big deal.

He was gross.

It was just David. Beginner's bad luck is all.

Sandy wished Linda would reach for her. She wanted to be held and kissed but she couldn't ask. It didn't work like that. It had to be Linda who reached, and Sandy who allowed.

Sandy felt miserable, a confusing unhappiness that tugged and nagged, just wouldn't let her be. She rolled over on her stomach and began to weep.

"Are you crying?"

Linda set her hand on Sandy's back.

"Don't cry."

Linda pulled Sandy into her arms and held her for

Prom

a long time.

Linda smiled fondly at the photo. "So, you see. After the commotion stopped, I gave Sandy a little good night kiss. I was kind of sleepy but it blew my mind, hey I woke right up. She was so *eager*. I decided I'd keep right on kissing her until she stopped first."
"How competitive of you."
"Sometimes you're not very nice."
"Well?"
"Well, I lost. I couldn't hold my breath that long."
The lovers sat quietly for a moment, the photo between them.
"Linda?"
"Yes."
"It's very pretty, I suppose, if you leave the story like that."
"I like it that way."
"You know how I am though, about the truth."
"Yes I do, Caroline."

The last time they spoke was back home in Milwaukee again.
"And what am I supposed to do, become friends as though nothing ever happened?"
"Nothing *did* happen!" Sandy claimed.
"Seven years is nothing?"
"Yes, seven years is something. We were roommates, and friends. I'm not saying that isn't something!"
"We *loved* each other!"
Sandy looked at her and quietly insisted, "You know, Linda, maybe you're *that way*. I'm not, I never have been, I never said I was. The thing is, if you really loved me, you'd accept him. If you gave him a chance, I *know* you would like him."
Sandy grew more frantic: "What other man ever noticed me? I'm in the lab most of the day. He's not perfect, I never said that, but he is kind to me. More, he wants me. Do you hear it at all? He *wants* me. He wants to marry me. Why can't you be happy for me? You know

my parents, you grew up with me. They've been planning my wedding from the day I was born. Every year of my life, they've placed a gift in the hope chest that was passed on to me from my grandmother. Why do you make it so hard? You think I could just tell them I can't get married? *Huh?* I can't get married because Linda is in *love* with me. Do you think I'd be willing to hurt those people who've given me everything? *What for?* Don't be so selfish, we're not kids any more. Grow up!"

"You think I can't give you everything that they can? That he can?" Linda was bawling by this time; she knew her voice was out of control. She knew it scared Sandy, but she no longer cared. In fact she was glad. She felt like punching Sandy in the face until she came to her senses.

"I wish it was done with right now, everything all settled. I wish I was already far from you in California. I wish I was in my lab, and he had his practice all set up. I wish more than anything that I didn't have to stand here in the freezing wind listening to you yell at me."

"You can't hurt me!" Linda was hollering. "You'll see. I'll have it all. I'll have everything: a house and a car and a dog. . ." she no longer cared if she sounded ridiculous, "but I will *never* marry any fucking man to get it."

Sapphire Mountains

It was the big earthquake of 1959. They all remembered it, the biggest event in ages. LIFE did a full photo spread.

For Caroline the Year of the Big Quake was the Year Grandma Died.

The two forever joined, one could not have happened without the other. The scope of both immense, sudden. The changes incomprehensible, some dramatic, some so subtle they went unnoticed for years—when discovered, they always pointed back to the crumbling of what had seemed solid under her feet.

She was nine years old, it was August, unthinkable that Grandma should die.

Caroline stood on Grandpa's grave, next to the freshly dug one, wearing the dark blue, black and white checked dress that Grandma had stitched for Caroline's birthday earlier that year. It had little edge-trimmings of black velvet on puckered sleeves.

Caroline stood on Grandpa's grave sucking the hem of her dress, watching her grandmother's coffin being lowered into the ground. She remembered most vividly Ev turning suddenly toward her, harshly whispering:

"Get off of your Grandpa's grave!"

Three days later it hit.

The shaking itself Caroline never registered, but she knew from the snatches of her parents' conversation, the radio announcer's hysterical pitch, that the earth had shifted under them. She knew that highways had collapsed, that where a mountain had stood the previous day there now was a lake. She understood the meaning of that big new word: geography. They said *Montana geography will never be the same.*

And she knew that Grandma was dead.

Sapphire Mountains

Sapphire Mountains. Bear's Paw and Bear's Tooth Mountains. The Crazy Mountains. Those were some of the names Caroline's grandma had taught her, way back then. Maybe everything important Caroline learned as a child, Grandma taught her.

"It sure does get cold in here, Girl," Grandma's voice would greet Caroline as the girl snuck into the big bed.

"Girl," Grandma's voice in Caroline's mind all these years later; "Girl," and Grandma stroking Caroline's head even when there was no fever.

"When you were born," one of many stories late in the evening. "When you were born, they brought you to her, a fresh little bundle. Ev just pushed the nurse away. She said, 'I'm too tired!' and went back to sleep."

Grandma said it as though she needed to explain this to herself; perhaps if she said it enough times it would make sense. She talked as though she didn't remember that Caroline had been that little bundle.

"So, I decided that you would be my little girl. Right then and there. Now don't you go blaming Ev. Who could blame her? It was too much for her, but there you were: the spitting image of those boys when they were born, too. Don't ever say a word of this to your folks, a person can't blame them. But I looked at you and knew you were special.

"After the car crash with the boys, Grandpa and I had to move in. This was the boys' room, was their room up 'til then. I don't know where they were planning to stick you in this little house.

"Oh, what do I know, an old lady like me. Sometimes I try to imagine what it would have been like if they were with us, your brothers. I try to think: now how big would they be, how old by now? And you know what? It's real hard to remember them any more. And that's strange, because when such an awful thing happens, you just know your heart will never heal. But it does, Girl, it does."

Maybe Grandma thought Caroline was asleep by this time, because she was talking very softly. Maybe she kept on talking anyway because she was an old woman and no one else would listen.

"What happened to their stuff, the boys' things? I always wondered. We moved in the day after they put them under, Grandpa and I. He was already full of the cancer—though he managed to go on for another three whole years.

"I wondered where did their bunk beds go? Where were the toys? Just like they had never been here at all. You know, I have never heard Ev or Kendall speak those boys' names since. As if silence mends grief.

"I don't know Girl, maybe it does. It's never been my way.

"Ev so big with you on top of it all, and she barely got a scratch on her. Lucky, she was. And Kendall, he has never been the same since, though being his mother maybe it's wrong for me to say, but that one had a mean streak from day one."

Caroline peeked up at Grandma, the wrinkled hands gesturing, the pale eyes watery.

"Now I know you'll never say a word to them, you're such a big girl. Ev, she didn't mean to push you away. Girl, you were a real pretty baby: pitch black hair like a shiny bird, it was so fine that little bits of your scalp showed right through, already you had your ma's dark skin." Grandma's hand would be resting on Caroline's skull like a faith healer's.

"Maybe you don't believe my word, that you looked like your ma at first?" Grandma asked, and went right on.

"Oh, you were such a bitty thing. I thought it was 'cause Ev stopped eating after the accident. How can you grow a baby when you won't eat?

"I remember when the boys were born, your parents kept them in their own bedroom all night. First it was Kenny, then Robert a couple years later, so proud they were of those babies. When we brought you home from the hospital, it was *me* that held you in the back seat all wrapped up in a big quilt. Ev and Kendall were quiet in the front. We left Grandpa home—oh child, don't you remember him?"

Sapphire Mountains

Caroline shook her head, but Grandma was staring off into the dark room.

"That man was a grump! Maybe I shouldn't say it. But everyone talked, what a stingy old codger." Grandma laughed a moment at her bravery.

"Well, then bless him, he got his. He was a hard man, girl. He and your Pa, two of a kind. I don't know what makes a man like that, he was always that way, long before the cancer got to him. Pity me! Married to him for more than forty years! I can't help but think that he's at peace now, that we did our time together: now it's done.

"I don't know. I'm just an old lady. Don't ever forget that you were special to me. They didn't want the crib in their room. Don't blame them, my girl, try to understand. I would have brought it in here, with Grandma and Grandpa—wouldn't that have been nice?

"But no, Grandpa put his foot down, he wasn't going to have his beauty rest disturbed by any old baby crying. The meany! So I'd be lying here every night, lying here and just waiting—listening for any little sound from the crib stuck in the living room. Let me tell you, you didn't cry much! Nothing like when your dad was a baby! Yes, he did, he and his brothers were real night screamers. They'd be wailing like the end of the world. Maybe Grandpa remembered that.

"Well, at the first whimper, I'd scoot up to get you some milk. In the beginning, your ma would get up too, come out in the kitchen—she did it once or twice. I'd be standing in the kitchen, testing the warm milk to my wrist. It was funny, me being in her house. I didn't want to be stepping on her feelings. She'd just look at me like a sleepwalker, mumble she thought she heard one of the boys, then she'd head back into her room, as though she never even saw you tucked in the crook of my arm."

Crocks of Kraut

If I walk down the steps I can get to the crocks of sauerkraut, but I can't reach the light, and there are salamanders down there.

Salamanders; that's what the nuns call them, because of their yellow-spotted backs. Kids here laugh if I try to call them salamanders instead of lizards.

We pick them up and put them into an old milk tin. A whole bunch will fit. I don't like to hold the pail when it's full, though I don't mind picking them up one by one. Grab them by the tail, throw them in. We take the tin bucket and feed all of them to the chickens. Our mom tells us to do this.

That's during the day; now it's dark except for the bit of light that sneaks in under the door from the kitchen. I have to sit here. I don't know why. My father is mad about something again.

What I really want is sauerkraut from the big crock. That crock is bigger than me, and that's a lot of sauerkraut, especially if you remember how it was to make it. First scrub out a big enamel crock; then pick every cabbage from your garden, then shred them. This takes a very long time, and makes less kraut than you would think. What I don't like is that my mother says it has to cure. You can't eat it right away.

Some days when it's very hot, and my mother is down here putting clothes through the wringer, she goes over and takes the heavy rock from the round wooden top, takes the white dishtowel off, and says, "Let's see how this stuff is coming along."

Then she dips into the crock and pulls some of it out. I try to reach in too; she slaps my fingers away.

"Dirty hands could spoil that whole crock!"

She gives me a small sample anyway.

Crocks of Kraut

If I shut my eyes I can taste it now. It's almost an awful taste, especially at first, but then it's not. It doesn't taste like cabbage at all any more, it's a sour taste, it's a taste in your throat: sharp and salty. Cool.

Carefully my mother puts the cloth back, then the round wooden cover, then the stone weight. "Needs more time to cure."

"Why do you put that rock on top?"

"Gotta keep it under brine water. Gotta keep the cover on all the time. Contamination. Could spoil the whole batch."

Then she's back at the wringer: the diapers, overalls, and towels.

Now she's not down here, but thinking about those crocks of kraut makes me feel better, not so scared.

I think about the pears from the orchard put up in jars in the next room. But I'm not going down the steps in the dark.

I think about how hot it was today and remember choking on the tractor fumes, and the soothing smell of the fresh cut alfalfa, and how the air above the fields was so shimmery I had to turn away, and how carefully I measured the time my father, all the uncles, and my brothers would be out in the field and it would be just us girls, except for three o'clock when my mother sent me down the path with a big canning jar full of water, ice cubes and a pinch of salt for the men.

It was a rare day, with the men gone and us girls watching the vegetable stand. When my mother looked into the gray metal cash box before dinner she said it was a good day too. She bundled into rubber bands the dollars we got from hawking sweet corn to vacationers traveling Highway 12 to Wisconsin Dells, and stuffed them into her hanky drawer.

"What's a vacation anyhow?" I asked, though my sister told me not to.

My mother squeezed her lips tight. "That's for city folks."

I think of sweet corn and how I'm not tired of it yet; I could eat some now, the pale ears my brothers scorn. I'd have it dripping with butter, almost too hot to hold.

I think of the customers at the stand, those ones all the way from Nebraska who gave me a nickel tip and one for my little sister and I ran in right away and put it in my orange bank, and I didn't tell my mother.

"Don't be begging," she warns, bringing up full bushels from the field just after the sunrise picking.

I don't tell her about the men who stare at me while I fill the bag either.

"How much?" they ask, looking at my dusty, mosquito-bitten legs.

"Three dozen for a dollar."

"How old are you?"

I don't know what to say; they say Speak up girl, and I'm afraid I'll cry.

But mostly it was a good day and I was happy alone on my rope swing between customers, singing "Ricochet Lover" again and again. I didn't go looking for my mother, searching the potato patch or down here in the cellar. And later I filled the largest metal tub with water from the cow tank for my sisters and me to soak in the shade.

During the day I go down the cellar steps sitting on my butt, though it gives me slivers sometimes, one stair at a time. Standing up I know I could slip between the spaces and crack open my head on the cement at the bottom.

At the bottom of the stairs is a little room, the Egg Room. There is a scale to weigh each egg, sandpaper to sand off dried chicken manure. My sister and I gather the eggs from the chicken house and put them carefully into a wire basket, but my mother does the sanding. People from the town or farmers who don't have chickens come and buy these eggs.

If you go down the steps, past the Egg Room, past the big furnace and through the heavy door, beyond the coal bin, there are shelves of canned fruits and vegeta-

Crocks of Kraut

bles. What would I have if I could eat anything off of those shelves?

Maybe the pickles, the dill of course, not the sweet ones.

Or the pears: real sweet, sticky, you can even drink the syrup if you're quick. If your mom lets you, if you say, "Can I have some pear juice?"

"Pour a little into each dish so everyone can have some."

But you can snitch some off of the top first.

I wouldn't have canned plums, not those.

I would eat corn, if I could have it the way my mother prepares canned corn, with a bit of flour, milk, sugar and salt.

There's beans and tomatoes, for making chili in the winter.

Sometimes she makes pickled carrots. Too sweet for me.

I can't have any of those things now; even if I could reach them, how would I open the lid? If I could open them I'd be in even bigger trouble than I am already.

Under all those jars of food are potatoes in a bin. We dig them in late summer, and they stay cool all winter. Every night it's my job to come and get a big pot full. Sometimes they start to grow sprouts, sometimes they get mushy and stinky.

One time I put my hand out to pick up a potato and there was a huge hairy black spider. I tore back up the stairs, panting: "There's a big big big big spider down there!"

They laughed and laughed. "You're not going to get out of chores that easy. You get back down there and get your potatoes."

I saw where I had left the pan. I looked to see if the spider was still there. I couldn't see it. It could be anywhere: it could be under the potato that I was about to pick up right now. It could have already crawled into the pan, and as I was carrying them up the stairs it could crawl out and get me.

I can't have potatoes right now, but if I did I would want them scalloped, the way we have them on Christmas, with tiny bits of ham hidden like presents.

LIZARDS/LOS PADRES

I think about Christmas and the Good Room where the Christmas tree stands. I sometimes sneak into the Good Room quietly and I lie on the stringy pink couch and listen to my older sister play the piano, and if I am very very still and she's in the right mood she'll pretend not to notice, and I can stay. I like watching her so serious, with her long fingers moving like a wizard's across creamy keys chipped like teeth at the edges. I watch until I can see the notes dance, except really it's the birds, brilliant cardinals and clumps of flowers on the wallpaper. Then I count all the cardinals I can see next to me.

Behind the phonograph cabinet where the Christmas tree sits, is hidden the black metal clarinet case. When I'm very brave I look into it and remember the times my mother used to play, but then she'd stop and say the reed was broken or she was too old but I should have seen her in her high school marching band uniform.

"Clarinets sound funny," I told her once.

"It's a German sound, an unusual happy German sound. Get out of the Good Room now."

The harmonicas are stashed back there too in an old jewelry box, because she didn't like jewelry anyway, she said. He said she couldn't throw money away on an old harmonica and she shouted that she made money too and would have one nice thing in her life. But now she won't play. She tells customers that she had so many kids because she wanted to form her own polka band, but I don't like polka music.

I like to be here alone, watching the bulbs color the ceiling blurry blue, orange, green. Red.

Somehow the paintings look less spooky in the colored light. The bearded men must be saints or why would my great-aunts, The Nuns, have painted them? I wonder how men that angry could be saints, and worry they will fall off the wall and pull the plaster with them. I never look at Jesus, he's always waiting when you come in, right over the doorframe, like he might spit on your head or yell at you for letting his crucifix get so dusty.

Crocks of Kraut

The baby pictures over the piano are more interesting, the way my mom arranged us on the wall in the order we were born. We're all clean like this room that's kept nice for company, with its matching brownish-pink sofa and chair edged with wooden trim where I always whack my head when I tumble off the end with my sisters.

One time when I had to sit down here, they left the light on and I read all the old newspapers. I even read Ann Landers which they don't want me to. But the light isn't on, and I can't reach up over the stairs to the string. If I did turn on the light, my father would see it.

There's a dart board down the steps, for in the winter. My brother Spud likes to play; he's so quick, he grabs the dart right after I throw it. One person stands behind the chalk line, throws the darts as hard as they can, and the other collects them. One time my brother put his hand out so quick the dart stuck deep into his knuckle. He went to the doctor. I never grab darts.

In the winter muskrat skins hang stretched tightly across metal frames along the rafters down here, over in that corner by the guns. My brothers walk across the ice to set traps for them in the marshy grass on the edge of the pond. Each of my brothers gets first a BB gun, then a hunting gun, when they're old enough. I don't care, I don't want a gun, just a jackknife like they get even younger than me. They use theirs to cut off squirrel tails to prove how many they shot.

If I had a knife I would whittle.

"Listen to her! She says she wants a jackknife for Christmas!" Hoots of laughter.

I haven't asked again for a knife, though I want it even more than to move up to a chair, off the long green bench that holds us little ones at the kitchen table. Everything's covered with that green paint, the bench and walls and the cabinets that my grandfather Hans built.

My father sits at one end of the table and pours salt on his potatoes and meat, yelling at us "Get me a fork," even though he's right next to the drawer and one of us girls will have to get up and walk all the way across the room to reach it. My mother told us girls while we scrubbed the supper pots how when she was growing up the women used to serve the men first, then sit and eat together in the kitchen.

"Except for serving the men I'd like that," I said.

The baby sits in a wooden high chair by my mother next to the flour bin. The flour comes in big cloth bags that my mother will sew into dish towels or dresses when they are empty.

From all that flour my mother bakes eight loaves of bread every week, brown and bursting out of the old tin pans. This week I watched her punching down a big bowl of rising dough, the same color as her pale stretching stomach that is beginning to peek out from her flowered smock again.

My mother framed one towel and hung it up; maybe it's not a towel. She says she embroidered it when she first married, now it's a faded blue "Home Sweet Home". The plaster Virgin Mary stands high in her corner shelf, sadly observing the endless sinks full of dirty dishes, garden vegetables waiting to be rinsed, chickens to be plunged into boiling water, to be plucked and gutted, dirty hair to be washed and rinsed with vinegar. Mary never says anything, I wonder don't her hands get tired held out like that all day? At night does she soak in the sink where we climb up and wash out foot cuts? Does she dance with the mice that run in and out of the burners?

I think of the pink plastic font of holy water at the door, nailed through the layers of green paint to the wood that must still exist underneath. The full flystrips hanging from the light. Then the dreaded rack of rosaries tangled up in each other. The barn-clothes closet: ripped sloppy sweatshirts, worn blue jean jackets, heavy boots still crusted with manure and mud always falling out.

Tonight before I was sent down here my mother was scrubbing the floor, and I watched and wondered how she could tell the dirt from the stains on the mismatched linoleum. I wanted to ask her once again, why do we have to do this, the sweeping, the boys' manure tracks—we could do it all day, and it still wouldn't be done. But I didn't because she was scrubbing, and tears were dripping right into the dirty water bucket, and she doesn't cry often.

We all kneel on this floor, but the boys just do it for rosary every night. I hate it, I know that if there was a god he would have answered my prayers a long time ago and made it so that we wouldn't have to say the rosary every night. I hate it before we pray, and while we pray with my father yelling for us to be louder, and stopping to hit one of us, and then after it's over more hitting for not speaking loud enough or stuttering.

"H-H-H-ail M-M-M-ary."

"Say it again!" My father bellowing to my youngest brother, his hand raised, with that half smile of his.

Sometimes we come down here in the middle of the night or day, all of us, and pray while outside the rain and wind swirl and howl around the house and rattle the windows. "Tornado Watch!" my parents shout, running around grabbing kids, the clouds fierce, leaves and dust spiraling like in a big witch's kettle. They say if we pray hard enough the tornado won't touch down on our farm. I wish everyone would just pray to themselves so I can concentrate, because even though I'm scared I'm also very curious what it would be like to float away to Oz.

My mom warns me about tornadoes, and strange men in cars along the highway and at the County fairground, and getting lost in the city.

"That's an order. I gave you an order."

I'm not stupid or lazy like my father says; sometimes I can't do it. I don't want to get hit. When he finally leaves me alone I begin to mop the hardwood floor. Then I dust the two big oil paintings from the convent. I run the cloth first over the one on my father's side: it's Jesus, and he's still bleeding pretty bad from his head but it doesn't come off on the rag. Next I do Mary on my mother's side; she's holding her heart out to show me like a kid does a scraped knee; I dust it for her. Then I shine the mirror between the two paintings. I want to paint pictures for my own room, something fun.

Straightening the chenille spread on the bed I pull a few more of the nubby white tufts out; I like to see the tiny holes where they used to be attached. I do the bed quickly and shut the closet door so I can't see the thick leather belts hanging there.

Finally I take down the cross from over the holy water; I like the way it's made out of burnt matches all glued together and varnished. I want to collect matches and make a log cabin like this.

I go out of my parents' bedroom into the dining room. I know I shouldn't be in here but when it's all clean and polished and dark, and I pretend the veneer hasn't come loose on the bureau, and I don't turn around and look into the kitchen or the rooms we really live in, I can pretend we are a grand family in a grand house.

I like the thick dark door leading to the porch, with squares and rectangles of stained glass. The wood is carved in curls, and the deepest part of each curl is burnt black like lines of brushed ink. Before company my mother makes us run turpentine and oil into all the crevices and panels of that door; then we drag our rags across the boards along the edge of the floor and ceiling. When this is done it is very grand, especially when my mother with her head wrapped in a bandanna has crossed the floor on her knees and waxed the wooden planks. After she's done, if our father isn't around, she lets us little ones skate across the slick wood, polishing with our socks. I don't know why this is called the dining room, we eat in the kitchen.

Once when my brother and I were sent down to the basement to shovel coal and wood into the furnace, my brother took the the iron poker and heated it up in the fire until it looked like a hot coal itself. He pulled it out quick and pressed the red tip against the heavy wooden door leading into the coal room.

"Come on," he urged, "you should try."

Crocks of Kraut

See, it made this nice perfect black circle straight through to the other side of the door. It's not any fancy door or anything, just beat up, full of nails and stuff.

"Come on."

I tried, but I didn't do so good. I didn't like the burning smell.

My brother did another one.

"What are you doing? What do you want, the whole house to burn down?" My father was suddenly yelling, and whacking at our legs with the other poker.

I can hear the other kids climbing the stairs above me. The little ones will sit at the top by the radiator and listen to my older sister read from the *365 Stories of the Year* book. Afterwards my middle younger brother will bang his head until it bleeds or someone remembers to make him stop, on his same spot on the wall where the plaster has cracked and fallen away.

At the top of the stairs is the attic door. I never open it or go in there alone; someone might lock the door behind me and then I would have to sit on the very bottom step and try not to look scared so the moment the door opened again I wouldn't be teased. Everyone knows the attic is haunted: ghosts live in those cedar trunks and suitcases.

On either side of the attic door are my brothers' rooms, the big boys and the little ones. They sleep together two or three to a big metal-framed bed, and have closets with bushels of walnuts stored uncracked in feed sacks.

In the little boys' room my mother rubbed off a transfer picture of Little Boy Blue Come Blow Your Horn; right onto the wall, she must have done it before the wall got so crumbling and stained especially from the apple cores that hit it before bouncing into the basket.

We girls have to fix the beds once a week, though we don't often change the old yellow sheets that smell like ammonia.

In the long hallway outside their room the little boys and I roll marbles to knock down enemy soldiers, with Tinker Toy and Lincoln Log forts and stations. The stairway rail is a white fence, or stanchions for us little cows; we line up with our heads stuck between the slats, mooing.

If my older sister is done now with the reading, she will be in the big bed with the chipping pink paint, already under the Wedding Ring feather quilt. There won't be any girl in the middle. They'll fall asleep playing 'what would you eat if you could have anything'. Or my younger sister will twist my big sister's ears and bop her nose playing juke box, and my big sister will sing country then switch to rock and roll, quietly. They won't be able to wait for me.

Those holes are still burnt into the door down there.

Maybe I have to stay here all night. Maybe they forgot about me. I know there's a ghost.

Killing Mice

"Aren't they just the cutest little things?" Stacy asks as she points at the shiny eyes peeking out from behind the fridge.

"Adorable." Caroline nods. Stacy finds everything cute or romantic. Secretly Caroline is plotting to buy some D-Con. Later she will tell Linda, "I couldn't tell Stacy or she'd never consider subletting her place to me. I feel like a creep, a desperate creep."

"I don't even want to discuss this with you. I have a very nice home which I bought with you and the boys in mind. If you want to choose to live in those crappy places, I don't want to hear about it."

Caroline can't tell if it's decent: clearly too small, one large room, the converted bottom half of a house. Its primary attraction is that she stands a chance of getting it.

"Looking at them close up," Caroline agrees again, "I guess they *are* cute."

Looking at them closely, Caroline plans where to put each box of poison. No traps, she can't set them, always the wire snaps back on her fingers, and then the corpse to dispose of.

It is the image of the mice climbing across her bed, finding that trail in the morning across the sheets, and chasing them away from the leftover breakfast dishes: she knows she wants them out before even bringing in the first of her belongings.

"Oh, and how are the mice?" Maybe Stacy will never ask.

"Stop worrying about housing," Linda told Caroline. "Let's get away, drive up to the cabin for the weekend. It'll be cold, but private."

Killing Mice

In coats, sweaters and long underwear the lovers watched whitecaps on Lake Michigan, and the formations of birds above it. They climbed the dunes. Caroline tried to charge up, getting halfway before sliding back down again. She held her hand up to quell Linda's laugh; on the second run she made it. Linda laughed and hugged her; she was shivering from the sharp lake breeze.

"Let's take the fire road into the woods, it'll be warmer."

On the way they played silly word games, and touched at every excuse.

"Oh, look." Caroline picked up a branch from the path. Linda wrapped an arm around her. Caroline ran her finger lightly across the one leaf that still clung to the branch, all of its parts gone except for the lacy skeleton.

They circled and ended back at the dunes. Linda playfully pushed Caroline into the sand; they started rolling down the dunes. Linda caught Caroline and held her. Working her hand through the outer layers, she began to rub her hand across Caroline's warm back.

"Cold!"

They stopped laughing and listened to their breathing and the waves.

"If it could always be like this," Caroline said quietly.

"It could," Linda replied. "I want you; make a commitment. Come and live with me. We'd have this every day."

"What about school, work, and the kids? Or money? And that's just for starts. Be real, Linda."

"I love you. That's real."

Then they had a vicious fight about what was real, and rode back to Madison in silence.

After Caroline picks up the boys and returns to their apartment in the project she finds the mailbox is empty. It still hasn't come.

"It's not our job to search for it," the central post office claims.

"But my check—"

"I'll give you a food bank referral, 'bout all I can do for you," welfare tells Caroline.

"Is that going to pay the heating bill? Laundry? Gas, so I can drive to school? Sanitary napkins?"

"Well, borrow from a friend."

Caroline politely bites her tongue, and hangs up.

"How much do welfare workers make?" Caroline asks her buddy at MATC*.

"Not much," Donna answers.

"What is much?"

"I don't know," Donna rolls her eyes. "I'm supposed to be too stupid to know what a poverty line is, and how much below it welfare mothers are."

"Who's she kidding? Who am I going to borrow money from?" Caroline asks. "My mother would give me a lecture with a small loan, and then scrimp herself the rest of the month."

"You can make a tampon with toilet paper, if you're clever you can," Donna advises as she takes a tofu and sprout sandwich out of a recycled plastic bag. She lays half of it in front of Caroline. "Now, a diaper isn't so simple. The laundry can pile up. I just squeeze my daughter into clothes I've set aside because she's outgrown them."

"I could ask my lover, but I think I'd rather starve first."

"I'd avoid it, especially with someone who's always had it easy." Donna shakes the empty crumbs off the plastic bag, folds it, and pushes it into the pocket of her down vest.

"She already loaned me money for school. The classes don't run with the public school schedule, it was borrow money for childcare or get a part time job. I knew if I took another minimum wage job I'd never get through school."

"It's a conspiracy," Donna assures her. "Finish school."

---

*Madison Area Technical College

Killing Mice

"I'm paying her every month. She says it's no big deal, that I don't have to. But I have to. And with my check two weeks late I have thirty dollars to my name."

"Can't they stop that check and issue a new one?"

"First thing I thought of. Would welfare be so sensible? Listen to this, it would take them two weeks to issue a new one, meanwhile if the old one showed up I'd have to destroy it."

"Why don't they just line us up and shoot us? Be cheaper." Donna picks up her books. "Are the boys home this weekend? If not, I'll come by and study with you."

Caroline walks, with a brisk careful stride, the icy sidewalks over to the elementary school, treasuring the time alone. The sun is bright, but the wind cold. She wonders about Donna. Why does Linda dislike Donna so much? She only met her that one time at dinner. Linda couldn't explain it herself, finally dismissing the subject: "How can you like someone who doesn't want to be around your boys, Caroline?"

Dear Mail Carrier, Caroline begins her mental hate letter:

For some reason you decided I didn't live here. I don't know why. Now my check is lost somewhere in the central post office.

"Little mistake," *you say. "Sorry about that." To you, it's just one more piece of gray paper shaped into an envelope, with another smaller piece of blue paper inside.*

After covering my rent I skimp by until the fifteenth; this time I've had to stretch that amount the whole month . . .

. . . I know this is senseless, not your fault. What is one mail carrier going to do? I'm just a name on a locked box screaming back at you.

Meanwhile Linda sends brightly wrapped roses almost daily. Caroline, answering the knock quickly because of the bitter cold, finds these expensive winter presents on her front step. Carrying the flowers back in the house and arranging them in an old juice jar, she angrily reminds herself she hasn't told Linda about the missing check. Still the sheer number of flowers seems an insult. She feels like she's being sold something. The cards that accompany each bouquet vary from amusing cartoons to deeply romantic scenes of sunsets, to arty imitations of ethnic crafts; and though she spends almost every other night with Caroline, every card speaks of Linda's longing to live with her.

"Is that what you want, Caroline? Marriage?" Donna asks her when they pause between Algebra problems.
"I'm married already. To the government."
"Don't buy it," Donna urges. "Since I was fourteen, I've worked. Hard. For years I took care of other people's children. I mothered the offspring of mayors, lawyers, professors, plumbers—you name it. I liked it OK, but I couldn't raise my own girl on that income. So, now I go back to school, and all those people whose kids I raised while they were making damn good money have got the nerve to bitch about welfare mothers. They can shove it. When I got pregnant with Chelsea, some of the hippest people in town told me to my face that only women with X amount of money should be allowed to reproduce. A woman with a source of income, they mean a man of course. I never figured out what makes the rich uniquely qualified to parent. Then I remember, shit, they don't *raise* their kids. Christ, Nancy Reagan's inauguration gown cost more than what I've lived on in the last two years."

When Caroline first moved out of the hippie collective one-bathroom household (ten adults, five kids and who knows how many crashers) the housing project seemed like heaven. She was afraid to put anything up on the freshly painted walls. The boys didn't want to sleep in their own room, because they had always shared one with Caroline. Caroline insisted they would get used to it.

Killing Mice

Now, six months later, she begins to notice that the tiles in the bathroom are always damp, mushy even, under her feet. *Gotta remind those boys to clean up after themselves.* One morning when she goes downstairs to fix breakfast for the kids, she opens the cabinet and notices all the packaged food is soaking wet. Rivulets of water run down the edges of the shelves. Caroline quickly pulls the boxes out of the cupboard, then crawls up on a kitchen chair to peer about. The bathroom is directly over these cabinets. She throws away the food and tries not to think about the cost.

When Caroline calls the project office, they put her on hold.

"Don't put me on hold again," Caroline begs the receptionist. "It's an emergency."

"Oh, that's been a problem in all those units. We'll send someone out."

"When?"

"Well, it'll be either today or tomorrow."

A plumber shows up late in the afternoon, filling the place with the reek of pot smoke. "Yeah, these apartments are notorious. Bummer."

The next morning when Caroline goes into the kitchen, the rivulets still run; in fact they have widened considerably.

"We'll send someone out," the receptionist assures Caroline again.

"When?"

"I don't know. You'll just have to be there, won't you?"

"Look," Caroline explains as nicely as she can, "I can't be missing too much school. If you let me know when, I'll be here."

"We can just give them a copy of your apartment key, then you won't have to worry yourself." The Voice has settled it and is about to hang up.

"No, I, well, I don't really want men in my home when I'm not here."

"Don't be silly. The plumbers are bonded."

"I'll be here if you tell me when they'll arrive."

Caroline misses school. She waits all day; the plumber never shows.

The trickle is now a stream.

Linda, looking at it next morning, announces in disgust, "I'm not spending time here any more; come and stay with me. Why do you want to subject yourself to this? You can do better."

"Lay off, I'm looking for another place."

This time, Caroline goes straight for the Voice's heart. "Look," she says, "this is causing *serious property damage.*"

A plumber arrives ten minutes later. All the plumbers in town seem intimately familiar with the complexities of these apartments' pipes, "Oh, yeah, right, same thing as in number six last month."

The leak is finally contained, the walls and cabinet still damp and streaked with white trails across the wood and paint. Caroline tries to scrub the marks away. Then for several blissful weeks she forgets about the plumbing.

One morning Zack calls from the kitchen, "Mama, quick come here."

When Caroline reaches the kitchen, Skye is laughing and shouting at the drips, "Go away or my mom is going to kill you."

Donna arrives a few minutes after, to offer Caroline a ride to school. "Shit, look at that!"

Exasperated, Caroline slams the phone down. "They put me on goddamn hold again!"

"This is obscene," Donna says. "Do you mind?" She dials the phone. "Yes, could I speak to the director please? This is in regards to a question I have pertaining to some Housing Project property. Thank you."

When Donna hangs up, she says, "I've found you gotta go to the top. Someone will be right over. I'll take notes for you, see you later."

Caroline puts the kids on the city bus to school, and walks back to her place. A very angry woman is waiting at her door. It's The Voice, fuming because Caroline has gone over her head. She marches into Caroline's apartment in her pointy high heeled boots, wrap-

Killing Mice

ping her camel hair coat closely to her chest as though Caroline were the intruder.

"It stinks in here." The Voice sniffs disdainfully at Caroline as though the smell emanates from her, and opens the window.

"It's the leakage. I told you the toilet was leaking."

The Voice grabs a tall kitchen chair, and wobbles precariously on her boots while inspecting the cabinets with a flashlight. "This is serious! The ceiling is damaged!" The Voice glares at Caroline.

Grabbing the soup kettle off the stove, The Voice picks a breadknife out of the sink and stabs it into the soggy ceiling. Water rushes out, spilling into the soup kettle. The water reeks. Little bits of soaked plaster stick to the pot, stovetop and sink.

The Voice climbs down, and picks up the phone and dials long distance to some plumbers in Sun Prairie. Then she marches out, repeating, "You know, this place just stinks. Leave your windows open."

This time the plumber rips out most of the kitchen ceiling to get at the pipes. He rips up the tiles of the bathroom floor to get at the rest. The ceiling looks like an explosion has torn through it.

"Good luck," he says as he leaves.

The only kitchen light dangles, unusable. Wet plaster clings to the stove and cabinets; a fine dust coats the floor and marks the plumber's tracks across the rag rug.

Donna and Caroline are drinking tea after finishing their finals.

"Well, she just wants it all settled. She's afraid it won't happen unless she grabs me now."

"Don't do it. Look at the pressure you're under," Donna argues.

"I can't live here any more. They'll never fix the ceiling. Now the heat doesn't work either." Caroline pauses. "The only other option . . . but I can't seriously consider it. Cynthia told me again the other day that she'd love to take the boys."

"Cynthia?"

"Jerry's off and on girlfriend." Caroline looks up into Donna's puzzled face. "The boys' father. She's known them for years."

"Caroline, think about taking her up on it."

"Be without my kids? . . . then I could find a room in a lesbian house . . . oh, but that's . . . I couldn't!"

"Still—"

"Linda gets so pissed when I look at other places."

"Come on, why let her push you around? She keeps you in a little cage."

"I wish you liked each other. This weekend was perfect. Linda and I skied in the arboretum for hours. Everything was so fresh. Undisturbed. The snow was brilliant, the trees just sparkled with ice. It was magic." Caroline gulps her tea and hurries on. "We barely talked, just kept smiling and pointing. It was good to be outside, working up a sweat. I've felt so stuck in that apartment. Afterwards she massaged my legs. We drank wine . . ."

"That's just one weekend. What about the rest of the time?" Donna asks. "It's skiing you love! You'd be thrilled out there by yourself."

"She *loves* me," Caroline says stubbornly. "We'll end up living together in the long run, so it's just a little sooner than I thought."

"You sound like a pregnant friend I had in high school who got married at sixteen."

"Goddamn it, leave me alone." Caroline rises in a sudden fury. "I don't have money for first and last. I'm tired of money limiting all my choices—okay! I can't fight any more. I've told her I wouldn't be doing this now if I wasn't so desperate. She doesn't care, she's happy. I can't think. The damn lesbians in this town don't want to live with kids! All right, I don't feel like living with kids myself most of the time myself—and the straight women don't want to live with lesbians. I'm babbling, I'm tired, I don't know. I'm going home."

"What about Stacy's place?" Donna follows as Caroline heads for the door.

"That flake? Don't even ask." Caroline takes off down the street, winding her wool scarf around her head as she goes.

Killing Mice

Caroline remembered traveling years ago—the rats, not mice, rats like squirrels that hung about the plazas in Mexico.

She thought of the time she was nursing there, and a rat crawled across the bed towards her, attracted to the scent of breast milk.

Really though, she knows these mice mean no harm.

"I'm not allowed a cat. I'm not *allowed*," she said to herself. "I no longer know what's fair."

Caroline thought of those mice going out into the snow, or in the summer into the lush overgrown lawn; she imagined them searching for water, the poison makes them do it, search.

She pictured the dead mouse being eaten by an owl, and the poison travelling up through the food chain, eventually reaching back to her children, to her. But it was not only this, that it would eventually reach them. It was the cowardice that desperation brings.

In the end Stacy called to say she decided to rent the place to someone else, someone she had giggled about, said she had a crush on, someone single she said, because after all she couldn't see how two kids and an adult were going to live in such small quarters. Caroline hung up the phone and wept; of course it was small, but it was a place. It was cheap, *how dare you.*

Linda helped Caroline move her things into her Victorian at the end of the month.

Caroline still wondered about the mice.

Marsha: 1962

1.

Marsha has been around for years. We've always said:
"Hi."
"How you doing?"
"That's nice."
"Terry going out for Little League again?"
"Good. Good. See you at the game."

Not much more. I thought I'd heard that she'd moved here from Chicago. It must have been quite a while ago. My boy and her son Terry have always been in school together.

1962 was the summer I moved out from Roge. The step before the divorce. I was bored, you see, that's what I thought the problem was. I was thirty-three years old and didn't know how to do anything. Oh yeah, well, I painted a little: just portraits of my kids. And gardens. I grew big gardens of flowers. And cooking, I was a great cook. That and reading. I did read a lot. We needed the money pretty badly, so I cleaned house for the lady down the street.

Basically I was just a housewife.

Roge gave me the separation without much fuss. Maybe he didn't take me seriously, because later he fought like the dickens.

The main wall decoration in the house I shared with Roge was a photograph of me from our wedding. I was twenty. The picture made me want to gag. My mother had had it blown up huge for our tenth wedding anniversary. What could I say: "Mother, that picture makes me want to gag!"

So there it hung, that dumb grin on my face twenty-four hours a day. I found myself talking to that

Marsha: 1962

overdressed nitwit during the months before I moved out. Sammy, my little boy, caught me once.

"Mommy, why don't you like that pretty girl?"

That very picture is the one my mother pointed at in shocked silence, before the predictable gush of tears when I told her, "I'm leaving Roge."

While my mother was pointing and being dramatic, Roge was saying, "There, there, it's only a trial separation," and sending me the evil eye, like how could I hurt this poor old lady!

I mean, Roge never even liked my mother.

My mother had a snit over George, my own brother, letting me use his place while he was gone for the summer. I think she was mostly in an upset because he knew before she did.

"And what about the boys?"

I resisted saying that they would probably see their father more now than they did when we lived together.

"Look," I said to my mother, "I don't want to badmouth Roge, but I'm not going to live with him either."

Anyhow, maybe it was the scandal of Youngstown that summer, and I just didn't know it.

Marsha seemed to take on a whole new dimension after I moved into my brother George's place and got it all decked out for me and the boys.

It was the Little League's Annual Kickoff Potluck. There I was with the boys. There was Marsha and she comes over and we start:

"Team should be great this year."

"Yeah, looks like."

"Nice weather for playing."

"Good dip you made," I say sincerely.

"No, really, I don't cook. I hate to. Picked that up at Piggly Wiggly's."

Blah Blah Blah . . . we go on to routine conversations with the rest of the mothers. I've known them all since I was a kid. Nothing new to say. Feel like I've been sleeping for twenty years.

Nobody is mentioning the separation, but the way they are being silent about it is so loud I feel embarrassed. The thing is I know they can't figure out why I would leave; Roge is an okay guy. I mean he isn't exciting, but he doesn't cheat (well really he does, but I don't know about it yet) or beat up on me, which is a lot more than most of these wives can claim. And then there are the kids. Well, it must seem unexplainable. Roge doesn't make any money, but nobody would fault a guy for that in Youngstown. I mean he tries.

But then Marsha is back to talk to me. She talks until ten o'clock and it's time to go; I realize that I've never noticed Marsha like I do tonight. Everything about her seems fascinating. She does all these glamorous things. Like for example, she's divorced. And she's a real estate agent. Real estate seems so interesting. She talks my head off. I stand there and nod. She's pushing up her glasses and gesturing away with her hands as she speaks. I watch her hands.

Then Sammy is pulling on me.

"I'm tired, can't we go home now?"

I want to wring his little neck.

My big boy Neal comes up and says, "I'm tired Ma, let's go."

I'm stuttering goodbyes; my face is turning red. What's wrong with me?

The boys are quiet all the way home; the little turkeys better not give me any fuss about going to bed. I'm not concentrating on driving, I'm thinking about Marsha. About how well she speaks, how sophisticated she is.

After I get the boys in bed, and it's quiet, I drink one of George's leftover beers. The coolness of the beer I like.

I think: *I must be lonely, I barely know her.*

I just want a friend.

Well, why would someone like Marsha want to be friends with me?

And then I think, *Marsha happens to be a well-heeled woman. Educated. She took an interest in ME. Why shouldn't I have a new friend like her?*

I go to bed. I dream that I'm painting a portrait of Marsha. She's nude, she has her glasses on the whole time, she pushes them up on her nose while talking away about real estate. I'm trying to paint her, but the way her hands move distracts me. Then the boys come home,

Marsha: 1962

Roge comes in and says, "Oh, hi Marsha," and "Honey, what's for dinner?"

I wake up.

In the kitchen, I am remembering the dream.

"Mom! Hey, Mom!" Neal shouts into my face.

Oh yes, that's right, I remember my sons need breakfast. Did I take out these eggs? I start to break them into the frying pan . . .

"Mommy, you said French toast! You said we could have French toast! Not fried!" The six-year-old looks like he's going to cry.

I make them French toast and send them off to school. Two minutes later the door opens. It's Neal again, looking as sweet as can be.

"Mommy," he says, "this week at Uncle George's has been fun and everything, but you know, you've been kind of out of it. I was thinking maybe you feel a little down about Dad leaving us. Well, I want to let you know I'd be willing to call him and tell him to come and get us."

I'm floored. I don't know whether to whack the kid or hug him.

"Neal, it might not seem that way to you, but I'm doing great. I don't know exactly what's going to happen next, but things are changing. I know I don't want to be with your dad."

I look him in the eye, so he knows I mean business. "He's still your dad, but Neal, I left him. *I* left *him*. I'm not going back."

Then I hug him and he gets all embarrassed.

As I watch my oldest kid go out the door, I feel an incredible relief. I've said it. It's over. The marriage is over.

I start to wonder, *What am I going to do now? Well, maybe I could become a realtor.*

My mother interrupts with her daily phone call:

"How are the boys sleeping? How are you *sleeping?* I suppose you take good care of your brother's garden."

I make the mistake of mentioning that maybe I should become a real estate agent.

"What! Have you really lost your mind?" she says. "You? You hate real estate agents! Don't you remember that one that practically sold Roge and your place out from under you right after Sammy was born? Kicking a family out like that! All these years you've lived in crummy apartment after apartment. Who do you think is making a killing on those places? What are you thinking of anyhow, Roge is never going to let you work!"

"But Mother, I do work."

"All right, but honey, cleaning Myrtle Henning's house isn't really a *job*. Roge would have a fit, take his last little bit of pride away. You know he's done his best by you, can't help it if the plant lays him off. Shame on you— a real estate agent!"

I let my mother go. I guess she's right. I don't really like real estate agents.

But Marsha I like. I begin to wonder what she does all day. Next time I see Marsha, I'll just express a professional interest. I'll say: "So, Marsha, tell me, what does a job like yours entail?"

I wonder where she is right now. I remember that house over on Nineteenth and Sweeny has a sign out front for her company. I really need the exercise anyway, so I decide to stroll over. Maybe she will be showing it, and we can just say hi.

I stroll past. Yep, there's the sign.

I go slowly. The place is locked up. There's no car in front. What kind of car does she drive? I can't remember. Does she have a car? *Of course she has a car! A fancy real estate agent, she has to have a real nice car.*

I turn and go past again. No one there. Walk five blocks further, then try again. The woman next door finally peeks her head out, says, "Interested in the house?"

"Oh, God, no." I'm embarrassed. "No, just curious."

Then we recognize each other: we were in band together in high school. We chat.

I go home. What was I thinking? That she sits at that one house all day? What would I have said, anyhow?

Hi, gosh, fancy running into you!

Marsha: 1962

I bake cookies for the boys. Make a special dinner while I watch a bake-along show. Roge calls just before I go to pick up the boys.

Roge always calls at this time of day, and he always says, "Honey, if you're interested I could drop by for dinner."

"Roge, if there ever was a chance of us getting back together, which there is not, this phone call routine would wreck it for sure."

When I pick up my kids, it hits me: who picks up Terry, Marsha's son? Maybe she will be here tonight. Maybe I'll just go up to her and say, *Oh hi, hoped I'd run into you.*

No, no, I won't say that. I'll say, *Listen, I've got this great idea for the mothers of the Little League to raise money for the team. I know you don't like to cook, so why don't you and your kids come over and . . .*

This is ridiculous. I don't have any idea how to raise money. If I did, I'd do it for myself. Why am I thinking about this woman?

I get the kids. Marsha is nowhere in sight. I blurt out to Neal: "Who picks up Terry?"

"Huh?" he answers, "what are you talking about?"

"Terry, who picks up Terry after school?"

"Beats me, I don't know." Neal gives me his boy-are-you-weird look. "Oh yeah, I think he rides his bike."

All evening, I pay attention to my kids: I watch *I Love Lucy*, *Lassie* and *My Three Sons*. I supervise Neal's homework. I tuck them into bed.

I don't think about Marsha the entire next day, except briefly when I flip through the phone book for the plumber and happen to get the page with her agency on it. I jot down the number just in case.

That night is Neal's first game of the season. Marsha has attended every Little League game I've ever gone to. She has to be there.

I pick up Sammy and take him to the game with me. I bring Neal his uniform. He changes and hangs out with his team; Sammy plays with the other little kids hanging around.

Marsha is already here; I see her talking with Terry. She must be about forty years old. She has a seventeen-year old besides Terry. She's chubby. I can hear my mother saying, *She isn't really even very pretty.*

I don't know where to sit, I hang onto my purse. Then she sees me.

"Here, I even saved a place for you. I was looking forward to seeing you."

She's off and talking. I'm sitting and watching and thinking of all the things I wanted to say when I saw her again. I don't say any of them. This is how we spend the whole game.

Then the game is over, and Roge is there. I realize Roge has been there the whole time, and now he's standing next to me just like a husband. I try to stand a little further away. He just moves in closer, totally unaware that I wish he would evaporate.

Neal is all upset that his team lost.

"Oh, you lost?" I ask.

Everyone is leaving. Marsha and I linger. Roge lingers.

I know Roge wants to talk to me; I want to talk to Marsha. I'm not sure why Marsha is lingering. It becomes a waiting contest. I make up my mind: I'm going to do it. Suddenly, Roge is taking me by the elbow, all husbandly, and Marsha is saying, "Well, this was really nice."

Roge is waving goodbye.

Puzzled, I'm fighting back tears.

"Honey, let's take the boys out for pizza. I told them we would, just like old times. Come on, they're waiting for you," Roge is saying.

I turn sharply on him. "No, Roge! Not like old times."

I fire across the parking lot, across the field after Marsha, catching up to her by her car.

"Where's Terry?" I gasp.

She turns around, surprised. "Well, he rides his bike."

"Oh, that's right. Uh, I wanted to talk to you." I startle myself. "I mean, I mean, if I called you, would you talk to me? How can I get in touch with you? Should I give you my number, I mean would you call me if I did? I don't know what I mean."

Marsha: 1962

My face is scarlet.
The whole speech lies there between us.
Finally, all calm, she says, "Here's my phone number." She hands me her real estate business card with her home phone number scribbled on the back. I'm breathing again.
She looks me right in the eye. "If you don't call me, I'll call you. What's your number?"

I have her number. What am I going to say if she calls? I hope she calls me. I put the number in my underwear drawer for safe keeping.
She doesn't call on Friday, Saturday either. Sunday at five o'clock, I find myself dialing her number. She answers.
"Oh yeah, I was going to call you."
Why didn't you?
She blabs away.
Finally, I ask, "When can we get together?"
"Well, when are you available?"
"Me? I'm available all the time, anytime, I'm just a housewife."
We arrange to get together for dessert at my house—well, at George's house—Wednesday night, after the boys are asleep. Her boys are big enough to take care of themselves, she says.
Wednesday night, three whole days!
I do my housekeeping job on Monday. I work on being a good mother, and field calls from Roge and my mother all week
I get reports from Roge's buddy Jay, at Lucky's where he's a checkout clerk, that Roge has been drinking at the bowling alley every night for the last two weeks, and aren't I being a little rough on the poor guy—all this while my groceries are being carried out. I'm wishing that I didn't know everyone in Youngstown. Or that they didn't know me.
I shower and try to figure out what to wear. I change my outfit twice. What am I doing? There's not a spot of dirt left in the house to clean. Luckily, I baked the sponge

cake early this morning; the very thought of cooking makes me sick.

She finally arrives, bringing a pink bakery box which turns out to contain a New York Chocolate Cheesecake. I set it in the refrigerator next to my Betty Crocker spongecake.

Will she think I'm a hick if I offer her lemonade?

Settled in the living room, she tells me everything else I didn't know about real estate, all the good deals she's made this year. I nod, and ask lots of questions.

"My goodness, I never realized one could do so well in Youngstown."

"Oh yes," she replies, "with the University and all."

We are on the couch because it's the only comfortable piece of furniture in the room. She has her shoes off, and she asks if I mind if she puts her feet up, and I say no, and then she puts her feet in my lap. It all feels real cozy, natural.

We keep talking and I realize I've never talked like this before, ever, except that she does most of the talking and I mostly nod. Somehow I get my feet up too, and the cheesecake is gone. We talk about her divorce, and I make her describe Chicago to me. She says maybe sometime she and I could take a drive up there, just us girls. Suddenly she stands up and says, "Well, this has been just swell." And she's gone.

Just like that.

The clock reads way past midnight. Have I been dreaming? I clean up. I feel stunned. I change into my pajamas. I get into bed. I get back out of bed, go to my drawer, and get out her number. I dial it fast. It rings a few times at her house. Oh my God, I think, she might not be back yet. I don't want to wake her sons.

"Hello?"

What to say. "Uh, it's me."

"Oh." She doesn't sound surprised.

"Why did you leave like that?"

"I don't know. I was, oh, tired."

"I'm sorry I kept you up so late, I mean, we were having so much fun."

"Well, then let's get back together again."

We agree to go for pizza after the Little League game.

Marsha: 1962

Roge calls the very next day, as usual: "Honey, let's go to the game together. "

Then he whines, "I'm miserable."

I say, "Roge, you're not miserable, I got it from a very good source that you're at the bowling alley every night."

"Only because I miss you so much."

"Roge," I tell the man, "I have other plans."

So Roge says, real tough, that he's going to take the boys after the game.

"Good, please keep them for the night."

"Fine, I will!" he snorts.

The night of the game finally comes. Marsha sits on one side of me, Roge on the other. They exchange light chatter across me. Roge nudges me, slaps my leg every time Neal makes a good catch or gets a hit. I can't look at Marsha; she talks to me, but she seems more interested in the game than she did last week. I look at her sideways when she is absorbed in the game. She's taller than me. Her skin, it has no olive in it like my own. Fine blond hairs on her tanned arm.

She turns all of a sudden, dark brown eyes contrasting with the blond hair. "Did you see that?" she asks, all excited. Then she's quiet, and we just look at each other; embarrassed, I turn away.

"Yeah," Roge is saying, "that Melvin thinks he's the goddamn coach!"

I glare at Roge: *if I was a witch, you'd be a fly right now.*

Then the game is over. Neal is in a tizz again over losing. Roge is telling Neal how well he played, and Neal is telling his dad to "Get lost!"

I say goodbye to all of them.

Roge says, "Maybe later?"

"No."

Marsha takes my elbow and says grandly: "We're going to dine together."

"Well, talk some sense into her head," Roge advises.

We all laugh.

I kiss the boys. Sammy looks at me like I'm a monster.

Marsha orders the pizza, says, "I hope you like olives," gives me a glass of wine. I nibble a crust. She gobbles down her food. Her hand as she talks brushes my arm. Her foot touches my ankle lightly. I shift away.

I find myself talking to her, and she listens. I talk about the books I check out from the library, my garden back at the old house, and she's not bored. She says she'd love to see the pictures I did of the kids.

We come back to George's house and sit on the sofa. She doesn't ask can she put her feet up, she just does it. My feet are up too; she holds them, her arm curled around them comfortably. We can't stop talking.

I'm so tired, my eyes keep shutting. I almost want to fall asleep like this. I am afraid she will see how tired I am and want to go. She says she should go, but neither of us moves from the couch. She says, "I'm going to go." She still doesn't move. I notice how very quiet it has become. She sits up and looks at me.

She says: " . . ."

and like a fire alarm the phone goes off.

We both leap up! I grab it.

"What?" I shout into the phone.

It's Roge.

"The kids wanted to say goodnight to you."

"For Chrissake, Roge," I yell, "they should be in bed! It's too late for this!"

I hang up. For a second, I feel sorry for him.

She's standing right behind me. It's hard to turn around. She's quite close. I turn to say goodnight, but don't look at her face. Somehow, we get from this awkward moment into a hug; it's an embrace we get stuck in. When we stop, I will have to look at her, so we stay in it and stay in it. I am desperately holding on to her.

A warning goes off. *But it's not like we're doing anything.* And then we're kissing. We're stuck, hugging and kissing. I know soon we'll have to look at each other; what will we say then? What will we do? I'm afraid to let go.

Then Marsha stands back, and I see she doesn't have her glasses on. She looks me right in the eye and says, "Do you want me to stay or do you want me to go?"

Marsha: 1962

No words come out of my mouth, all I can think of is to reach out. I take her hand, we go into George's bedroom and lie on the bed in the dark.

As I lie there, I think, *I don't know what to do. What did I think I wanted?*

But we aren't doing anything anyway, so I think, *Good, maybe we'll just go to sleep.*

We lie there a long time holding hands, and we don't talk. Her breathing sounds like she's asleep. I feel strangely disappointed; I squirm a little, wondering if she might still be awake, but then I hear a little snore. I reach over and touch her. I mean to touch her shoulder, but instead my hand falls on the cotton crew material over what I quickly realize is her left breast. I'm too embarrassed to move it off, because I don't want to wake her up, so I leave my hand there for a moment. I notice she's not wearing a bra, but a T-shirt instead, and I notice how good her breast feels. I follow the curve down to her tummy. It's a nice tummy, so plump. It feels warm and smooth, and I begin to wonder what her skin would feel like.

I realize I'm not really sleepy after all; I'd like to watch her face as she sleeps. I've never seen a lady sleeping; but when I open my eyes, I see that *hers* are already wide open.

2.

"Yes, he's going out for Little League, wouldn't miss it for the world, and yours?"

This one, adorable, she is. God, how am I supposed to keep these names straight. Looks like some wholesome mother right off the TV set, married to Dick Van Dyke or that sort, except, no offense, minus the clothes budget.

But wait, isn't this the one everybody's buzzing about tonight, what's her name? Left her insipid husband, him I remember. Rob or Ron or something: Big

Mouth, know-it-all type, keeps her on a tight leash. Oh, boy, he must be squirming. Well, good for her. She's got my support, though no idea, I'm sure, of what it means to go around the *divorced* one. Well, who knows, half the time they don't go through with it.

"That's right Bill, Agatha, I'll take you through the place tomorrow at three. It's a gem."

"We'll be there, Marsha."

It never stops, do any of them ever dream how much I hate real estate? Though I make a decent living for a gal, it galls the men, they think I shouldn't be out doing it for myself at all, irks them, 'cause I'm good at it. Goes to show, don't have to love a job to be a pro.

Kids, husbands, Little League: can't we ever talk about anything else? Six years I've done this. Six years, I believe it: feels like a lifetime. Driving to Chicago now and then, it's not enough.

I want to have a conversation, I want a real conversation. I swear at one of these potlucks I'm going to get up on the table, throw bean dip at the men, and shock the ladies by revealing my past. *You certainly are not going to do any such thing! Look at you, now you've ruined your mascara. You've done it all these years, my dear, you can do it another six. Do you want to raise your own kids or not? Do you want to make a decent living?*

"I hate mascara."

"Delicious dip, Marsha."

Now, what the dickens is she doing here, I thought I was safely hidden behind the potato chips.

"I'm so embarrassed, I just can't remember names. You know how it gets, it's Mike's mom, and Kenny's, and I always end up calling you Neal's mother, in my head."

"Oh, that's fine. Well, I mean it's Darlene."

Okay, Darlene, tell me the truth, why did you leave your husband?

Well, for Chrissake why not ask, I mean my God, she's got to notice the gossip. Why not just out with it.

Gracious, I think she's actually staring at me, my mascara must be worse than I thought.

Regardless, we talk. I mean, we actually talk to each other. It's been so long since I've done this, I'm afraid I talk the poor lady's head off. Well, who would

Marsha: 1962

believe it? At the potluck! I'm actually having a good time, we're laughing like fools, and I mean real laughter. Then her kid, not the one on the Little League, he's too small for that, anyhow this tyke she calls Sammy, comes over and whines he wants to go home.

Darlene gets all flustered, tries to shush the boy for a moment, tries to pick him up; well, even I can see he's too big for that. She's reluctant to go, or maybe she's that type, you know how ladies can be, all polite and the like, don't know how to break off.

Her big son, Neal, comes along next and pulls Darlene away by the arm. "Well, this, I, gee, so, Marsha, well, it's been, maybe, see you, goodbye then."

I could have sworn she blushed, saw it as clear as day. Too young for hot flashes. I like this Darlene, odd way of saying goodnight though.

Driving home, it's hard to concentrate on the streets, my mind wanders, I hope that my oldest, Richard, isn't out cruising with his buddies, that Terry will be safe on his bike in the dark.

I think of Darlene; once I had a husband too, ages ago. He's proud of me—no, that's untrue, he's proud that he's been able to keep me in line even from a distance, a respectable mother for his boys.

What did he think? I would expose our boys to it? Never would have, though I wasn't ashamed; that's what's wrong with me in his opinion, well *was* wrong with me, now I'm supposed to be over it.

I never meant for him to find out.

Don't blame yourself, Marsha. You didn't dream he would follow you.

There were the others who didn't get caught.

Oh, Marsha, what about Isabel who got to see her daughter once a year at Christmas under close supervision? Or Delia, who snuck around for fifteen years to keep it hidden. Better you should continue, you've done well here, it's just until they grow up.

I could be dead by then: once or twice a year, visiting secretly when the boys spend the holidays with their dad. I want a life.

That night I dreamt of the apartment I'd had in Chicago after my husband left me, like it used to be: Mo, Bea, Isabel and I playing poker. The kids fell asleep on the couch. I pointed to the boys and said, "Now they're gone. Let's dance."

When I looked back at the poker players, they were skeletons covered in webs, the bones of their hands still holding the cards.

"You were out late." Richard Jr., almost a man, greets me at breakfast.

"What are you, the curfew police?" I ask in my tough cookie voice. They both report to my ex, even now, six years later: I'm not to be trusted. Richie in particular hounds me.

"Where's my breakfast?"

"Listen carefully: this is a refrigerator, here is a bowl, here is a spoon . . . "

"It's your job to feed us kids. A kid has a right to expect his own mother to cook breakfast," Richie lectures. I wish he didn't look so much like his father.

"My job—let me tell you what my job is. In fact, come on over to the office, do real estate all day until it's all you have room for in your head.

"Come on Richie, you're no kid any more. You'll be in college next year. It's time to learn to take care of yourself."

"I'm not going to college, I'm joining the army. By the time I get out, I'll be married, and my wife will make me breakfast. Until then, I expect breakfast from my mother. That's just a basic, God-given right. And if you were any kind of mother at all . . . "

I leave mid-sermon, popping my head into Terry's room on the way out. "See you at Little League, guy."

"Bye mom."

At work, between the phone calls, showing houses, talking to the bank, and that seller who's been trying to dump his dive for six months, I think of the trade-off again; is it worth it?

Marsha: 1962

I think briefly of Darlene, and resent her for reminding me. I wonder, was I dreaming last night? How could she be any kind of friend? Not like the gals back in Chicago: we knew who we were, and who each other was. Can she make me *think* in the way I'm lonely for?

She's a funny woman though, I could tell that right off the bat. To laugh again, wouldn't that be something?

"Marsha, don't you have Bill and Agatha at three on Sweeny?" Alice totters in on her heels with the mail to remind me.

"That's right. Okay, listen: anyone who calls, I'm out for the day. Thanks."

"Terry got Little League?" Alice asks. "That Terry is all boy. You must be proud of your little man."

After showing the house to Bill and Agatha, I sit in my car by the park. This wasn't a sale; well, I didn't put much hope in it. Those two are never going to purchase anything, they just like a new backdrop now and then for their arguments.

For some reason though, Agatha touches a nerve in me. My mother, she reminds me of. My mother, who even dead, I can't cleanly grieve for. Richard Senior took it that far. Not that I'm ashamed. I still don't get why I can't have a private life.

Sometimes I understand why all those women want to chat about the easy things, watch TV, have Avon parties. Sometimes I think I would gladly do it, if I could. Haven't I tried? Haven't I? Bea says one doctor found we're born like this. It's cruel.

There are times I know it'd be easier if I could date a man, maybe get married again.

Date? Oh my God, I must be depressed.

Then I remember the Little League game. Ever since Terry joined the team, he and I have been getting along better. I make it a point to go to all the games, heck, it gets me out of the house in the evening. Watching, I wish I could play. I was great as a kid, still am when Terry lets me help him practice.

"Now, Terry, just don't freeze up on bat this time, you're doing good son."

I turn toward the bleachers and see Darlene all by herself in a cherry-red sundress, looking kind of lost. "Hey, over here, Darlene," I yell.

Well, why not get some decent company for the game, it'll help me fend off the Dads who squeeze up and make indecent offers between plays.

I know it's not 'cause I'm any kind of looker either at a hundred and seventy-five pounds, pushing forty. It's the divorce, they think it makes a gal dying for anything. Save me, Darlene, save me.

"Saved a place for ya, got such a kick out of our gab session at the potluck."

Turns out, it's not such a great game. My boy's team takes quite a beating in fact. I can't say I pay much attention; it's that Darlene! That girl's a crack-up, not that she gets in a word edgewise with my yapping, but say, when do I get the chance? It's a rare pleasure knowing someone's really listening for a change.

'Course Ron or Rob, her booted-out husband, comes and plops himself down right next to us on the bleacher like everybody's supposed to think the two are all lovey-dovey again. Darlene's practically sitting in my lap to avoid rubbing sleeves with the guy.

I'm saying goodbye to the lady, and Rob or Ron has her in a tight grip; maybe he thinks I'm going to snitch on him for the time he put the make on me at a game last year.

On the way across the field the image of Darlene holding a fistful of cards, at the kitchen table with my poker-playing pals back in Chicago, pops into my brain.

You gotta be kidding.

Hey, she'd be fine. Put her in some pedal pushers instead of those J.C. Penney schoolgirl shifts.

Dream on. Can you see her bluffing against that gang?

Good point, I don't think that gal could bluff if her life depended on it.

I think they'd get a kick out of her, she'd like them fine too.

Yeah, as long as she didn't know.

Marsha: 1962

A tornado rips across the playing field just then: Darlene lands in front of me, panting like she just hit a home run.

"Where's Terry?"

Goodness, for a minute I panic: did something happen to him? Did he get hit by a car . . .

"I just sent him off on his bike."

Then Darlene is sputtering out a jumbled-up speech, and turning purple. I'm tempted to make her take a deep breath and start it all over again, that is until the words sink in. Why, the girl wants to be my friend. Never in all my years in Youngstown . . .

"Darlene," I say (she looks like maybe she's afraid I'm thinking she's a fool) "Darlene, let's get together. Here, take my number, give me a call. In fact, I've got my book on me, let me jot yours in here too."

That week we get so busy at the office I forget all about Darlene. I'm finally closing that deal on Sweeny. Not Agatha and Bill, of course. I heard through the grapevine they won't have me for an agent any more because they found out I'm divorced. Not the first time it's happened.

I'm pooped out by Sunday night. I finally settle down to a murder mystery in my room, and the darn phone goes again. I swear I almost don't answer it, *no I will not put a bid on that house for you tonight, drop dead.*

"Oh, Darlene, how nice you called. I was going to get in touch."

Darlene's so anxious, I figure something out right then, and it goes straight to my heart. The poor dear's friends must be shunning her; people can be so wicked when a lady decides to separate.

So I agree to come on over and chat with her that very week.

On Tuesday I get a note postmarked Chicago, from Mo, addressed to me at work where the boys won't pry:

LIZARDS/LOS PADRES

Dear Marsha; We're still playing weekly. Hoping you'll get up here in August. New partner, I'm losing money. She's one of us though, name of Connie, nice name wouldn't you say? Just joined the club, good kid, so, of course, guess who's charmed? Thought I'd tell you myself this time. The others tease, you know. They'll be spreading gossip.

There is a new little paper comes out. Just pepped the whole group of us up! I will show you next visit.

Issie lost her job. Tough year for that one. We're doing what we can to keep her with us. She's talking maybe finally heading off to her parents back in Alabama. Please, Marsha, drop the girl a line. Between religion, and hospitals, and with respect to you, ex-husbands, I've lost more than I care to name.

Your Dear Friend, Mo

I almost forget about Darlene's invite, so the last minute Wednesday evening I stop by the bakery and grab something that looks like the best in the house, and it costs it too.

I feel gloomy. Mo's letter haunts me: I want to be part of the gossip, I want to see the paper, more than anything I want to convince Isabel to stay; who can tell her better what it means to leave? Mo writes in code; I wonder, is it easier to live like this, knowing of them and their life, or to forget them all, like before, when I thought I was the only one.

"Where are you going?" Richard Jr. demands, as I dash into the house to change into a pair of slacks and a crew-neck.

"What is it with you, Richie?" I ask, quickly slipping on my canvas shoes.

"Don't call me that sissy name any more. Where are *you* going? It's not Little League tonight."

"I'm going to visit a friend, Richard. Gosh, who is the mother here?"

"That's what I want to know. Since when do *you* visit *friends*?"

Marsha: 1962

"You're beginning to sound an awful lot like your father, do you know that? I do not have to answer to you!"

I dig my wallet and keys out of my purse, and head for the door.

Almost fifteen minutes late, I finally get to Darlene's place. Still shaking with rage, I knock at the screen door. The humiliation: my own son treating me like a child. Sometimes I swear if it was just Richard, I'd let his father take him, and I'd go right back to living with the girls, having a gay old time.

Pink, that's what I see when Darlene answers the door. I hand her the pink bakery box, her face blushes a bright pink which almost matches the tiny pink roses on her shift. Now, I'm not big on pink, but at that moment, I confess, it made a pretty sight and I cheered up a bit.

"Lemonade?"

"Sure, sounds great."

"It's not much of a place I guess," she apologizes as she leads me into the tiny living room.

We sit on the couch, and before I know it, it's so easy to be with Darlene, I forget all about Richard Jr.'s behavior.

" . . . and then Agatha says, 'but Bill honey, this would be perfect for a little nursery—'

"he goes, 'a darkroom, that's what I'd put in here.'

"she says, 'a baby doesn't need any darkroom, what are you thinking?'

"he starts to yell, 'WE DON'T HAVE A BABY AGATHA—'

"she hisses back into his face, now remember I'm standing right there the whole time in plain view, 'That's right big shot! Because *you* are doing it wrong!' "

"Well, I couldn't help it, I burst out, I'm not talking about polite chuckles either, I couldn't stop, I started choking and coughing."

"And these are the same people who won't come back because they found out you're a divorcee?" Darlene asks, while she takes her fifth tiny slice of the cheesecake. "This is good, cheesecake you call it? It doesn't taste like cheese. Is it cheddar?"

"Some people act like you're a criminal when you get divorced. The wives think you want their hubbies, and the hubbies are always sidling up when they think no one can hear, inviting themselves over."

"You're the only person I've ever known who was divorced, except I mean, like movie stars." She admits it shyly, like she's not sure if it's polite to mention. "I guess I've always thought of you as being awfully brave. And lucky, though I don't know why. No dirty men's socks to wash or something."

We laugh.

"I've got the worst varicose veins. Mind if I put my feet up?" I ask her.

"Oh, goodness no, of course not."

The couch is so small that finally I plop my stocking feet into her lap, quite a relief to raise 'em.

"Do you play cards?"

"No, well I play Go Fish." Darlene answers seriously.

"Crazy Eights? Slap Jack?" I kid.

We crack up until we are holding our sides.

"I meant . . . " I choke back hiccups, "you know . . . oh dear . . . help . . . poker."

"You mean real poker?" she asks, a bit shocked, but admiring. "Marsha, you play poker?"

"Oh, honey, what a shame! I'll have to teach you."

"Me? I mean, do you think I could?"

Then I tell her all, no not all, but quite a bit, about my weekly game back in Chicago.

"Ladies, by themselves?"

"Exactly."

"That's so different."

I end up talking for an hour—I'm back in that tiny wood-paneled Chicago apartment, and Darlene's with me, and Mo still in her cabdriver uniform is trying to get the gang to throw in more chips, and Isabel is everyone's first choice for partner— stone face we call her— and Bea is running around serving beer and pretzels and forgetting to look at her hand, and as it gets later the downstairs neighbors rap on the floor (their ceiling) with the broom and holler "cut the noise up there or I git da cops," and then we shush for about three minutes each

Marsha: 1962

time before Mo gets us going again with stories from her day's work. And we know Lonnie downstairs will be in a funk about losing sleep but she won't fink on us.

I snap out of it, and look at Darlene. The kid has big tears running down both cheeks.

"What is it?" I ask, as it suddenly dawns on me: did I let her see Mo's haircut, the men's pants? Did she see Bea dropping into Isabel's lap between games for a kiss?

"I want to go."

"Where?"

"Chicago."

Without thinking, I'm so relieved that she's not crying because she figured it all out and is about to order me from her house, I suggest, "Say, maybe we could do a little trip sometime, just us girls."

She looks at me like I've offered her the world. "I've never been anywhere."

I watch for a moment as Darlene picks at a loose thread in her shift: a short, olive-skinned woman, with pitch-black wavy hair—who's she? Looking at her I panic, I can't breathe all of a sudden; what am I doing here?

I leave her house as fast as I can, I don't even remember if I say goodbye.

By the time I reach my driveway I'm so angry, yes outraged, I can barely open the garage. *I promised myself, I promised . . . ridiculous, stupid, sick pervert.*

My keys drop noisily to the floor, "Dang it!"

"It's after midnight!" A teenage voice comes out of the dark.

"You shut up or I will spank you. I don't care how old you are—"

The phone interrupts my threat. *Oh my God, has he called his father on me already?*

"Hello?"

Richard is standing behind me; I try to shoo him away so I can talk with her.

"Yes of course, we must. How about pizza after the game then?

"I did too.

"Good night."

I hang up, and my son grabs my arm; his breath stinks of beer.

I pull my arm loose, "What do you want? Let's just have it out."

"I want a normal family."

"In a normal family, you'd be grounded a week for drinking."

"It's normal to experiment with alcohol." He breathes all over my face, slurs, "I'm a normal teenage boy. I want a normal mother, got it, I'M NORMAL."

"Yes, you are." I shake my head at him as I go toward my room, tell him softly, "They say it isn't genetic Rich. So stop sweating it."

This is absurd. I can't have a friend even, I'm so abnormal that I begin to feel that way.
It'll pass, just like all the times before.
I won't see her any more.
I'd like to see her again.

During the week, the office slows down a bit. I finish the murder mystery; the spinster did it of course.

Terry and I practice catching.

"Mom, why does Rich get mad when you practice ball with me in front of the house?"

"He does? I didn't know. I guess he thinks it's weird for mothers to know how to play."

"He said he'd pound the shit out of me if I did it again."

"Are you scared?"

"You'd protect me. But why mom, why does he get his undies in such a bundy over everything?"

"It's hormones, Terry."

"I hope I never get them."

"Me too."

When I drive up to the game this time I feel sick to my stomach, maybe it's the flu, I haven't wanted a bite

Marsha: 1962

all day. I think if it's the flu, Terry will probably understand if I don't stay. I stagger over to the bleachers.

Darlene comes up to me, all smiles: she's wearing a white sweatshirt and plaid skirt. I mumble hi, and stare at my thumbs until the game starts.

I wish I could coach the team, they can't be as bad as they look out there, I mean who assigned Jimmie Hodges to first? Figuring out what I'd do if I were coach, I forget about Darlene sitting next to me, and about feeling sick. First thing, those boys would have some batting practice, that's for sure. What am I doing? What a dumb daydream, to imagine that they'd ever let a gal coach. A damn shame though, think what Mo could do with them, I'd like to meet the man who knows more—

"They called him OUT? I can't believe it!"

I turn to look at Darlene, "Did you see that?" Still pointing out to third, I really *look* at Darlene's face for the first time. Her eyes are almost black, they're so dark. Though the rest of the world might say her teeth are a bit funny, in that moment she's beautiful. She turns away, embarrassed. *God Marsha, how rude to stare.*

"Yeah, Danny's dad should stay on the bleachers, let the coach take care of it!" Rob-Ron's voice travels to me across Darlene.

You mean, that jerk has been sitting next to us the whole time?

Darlene and I both look at what's-his-name, then at each other; for the look in her eye at that moment alone I could fall in love with her. She's not going back to him.

Terry's team ends the game with zero runs. He's a good sport, but Darlene's son is huffing and puffing.

I don't feel sick any more, in fact, I can barely wait to get out of here, over to the pizza parlor. I'm famished.

"Let's scram," I say to Darlene.

Darlene's picking up her purse and giving instructions to her smallest son about pajamas. Her hubby puts a hand on her shoulder and says in a not very subtle whisper, "I'd like to get together later, honey."

Spare me.

Darlene looks at me for help, so I bow slightly to them both like the court jester: "We have plans," I say.

We hook elbows old lady style and turn to walk to my car.
The man looks puzzled a moment, then remembers we're just a couple of silly girls, and advises me, "Well, talk some sense into her head."
"Oh, I will. You can be sure of that."
Darlene and I laugh all the way across the playing field, arm in arm.

I don't know what I was thinking all day, I'm so hungry I could eat five pizzas. Once I've got food in my stomach, I get that same happy feeling I had last time with her.
Tonight she's more talkative.
"But what is it that you like to read?"
"Just stuff from the library."
"Tell me."
"I hope you don't think this is childish, Roge always says I am. Last time I went to the library, I was trying to find something I could read to Sammy at bedtime. It's very difficult you know, because he mostly wants to watch TV."
"Isn't it the truth? My boys too."
"This one book I loved as a little girl. Maybe you know it? I told myself Sammy would enjoy, it but he got bored by the second page, and so I decided since I don't have Roge there to tell me how silly I'm being, I would finish it myself. It's called *The Secret Garden*. Do you know it?"
"Yes. I do."

We return to her house.
"But then you're an artist!"
"Oh no, nothing like that. I dabble. It keeps me out of trouble."
"I want to see."
Darlene turns pink again, unfolds some drawings she's pulled out of a closet.
"Sammy, when he was a baby, finally sleeping. Looks like an angel, doesn't he."

Marsha: 1962

"Sure does. Wears off quick, doesn't it."

"Sleeping, he really did. Oh, and here's one of my mother, she didn't like it. Said it made her look old. And here . . . "

"What about this?"

"Oh, that's nothing. Just flowers."

"Darlene! I don't know much about art, but these are a joy."

She takes a rubber band off a roll of fragile yellowed newsprint, and lets fall to the floor a whole bunch of pastel drawings: roses, lilies of the valley, bachelor's buttons, tulips.

"I haven't looked at these in years. I did them when I was first married, before the kids. See, I grow flowers. I mean I always have, but not so much this summer. The garden is back at Roge's. A hobby. I like to draw them so I can see them bloom all year long."

We pass the sheets back and forth, looking in silence.

Finally she stuffs them away, shuts the closet door.

"Darlene," I tell her, "you have a talent."

"No," she says, "don't talk like that."

"Have you always done this?"

"As long as I can remember, well, when I've had the time. Not often since the kids. In high school there was this teacher, Miss Kintry, an old spinster, she worked special with me. She said she'd get me a scholarship, I should go on. Of course I never gave it a thought. I mean I was already engaged."

She looked at the clock, shut her eyes, I could tell she was exhausted. It was quite late.

"Let's talk about something else."

"What?"

"I don't want to put you on the spot. You know, I mean, I've left my husband. You're the only other girl I know who's done that. Well, why? I mean, can you tell me why."

I gulped, "Do you know why you left yours?"

She was so tired, the words were sleepy, like a girl staying up late at a slumber party.

"I can't explain it to anyone. They all think I'm going through a stage."

A stage?

Darlene continued, "It's, for all these years, I've been so, well, so bored. Maybe that's a childish reason like Roge says. My mother says there are worse things than boredom, like being divorced for example. I think I would just have gone on being bored, telling myself, this is it, this is all there is. I mean that's the first reason, the boredom seems to be growing, and when Sammy goes to school in the fall, I think I might go out of my mind. You know you really can't do anything even when they're gone all day, Roge would call a couple times, come home for lunch, then when he was laid off, he'd be home all day, and I'd have to wait on him hand and foot. Still, if it was just that I probably wouldn't have left all of a sudden."

Her voice is soothing. I want to keep listening.

"Well," I say, "so what was the second reason?"

"No," she turns red. "I can't say. It's very embarrassing."

She pauses, then pulls her shoulders up and glances at me as though relieved; she says softly, "I'll tell you, if you promise not to tell a soul."

I nod. "I'm good about secrets."

She swallows, then starts, "One day when I was cleaning, I decided to tackle the attic. A surprise for Roge, make a space for him to do hobbies in, I mean not that he has any hobbies, but I thought he might if he had the room."

She's quiet for a while.

"I don't know how to say it, I mean, in the attic I found . . . well, three big boxes . . . they were packed full. I mean, you don't know what it's like when you've been married for thirteen years and then you find . . . "

Oh, my God, is Roge homosexual?

"Those boxes were filled with dirty magazines, I mean, I've never seen anything . . . it wasn't just girls without clothes on, I mean they didn't have clothes on, though they didn't look like me . . . but, well, they were doing things you can't imagine. Men doing things to girls I never heard of. Every kind of lady, and some of little girls, I mean children. I can't say any . . . "

"That's horrible." I mean it.

Marsha: 1962

"No one knows. Not even Roge. I tried to stay with him, I did, for a month after, but I couldn't look at him without feeling like I had morning sickness all over again. I couldn't stand to do his laundry, wash his underwear. I couldn't cook his food. And I couldn't sleep in the same bed with him. Maybe I'm more innocent than I should be at thirty-three, but I couldn't bear the thought of spending the rest of my life with him."

It's silent for a long time then, as we lie on the couch, our feet tucked into each other's laps.

"Marsha, why did you divorce?"

"He left me." I look into her dark, soft eyes. "Darlene, I'm gay."

She smiles, her teeth showing in the dark. "I'm very happy, also."

The world is quiet around us, except for the faint night buzz.

"I should go." I finally say.

Darlene lies with her eyes shut, she looks so peaceful.

My head is spinning, I *want* to tell her something about it, my being gay, it isn't fair not to, I open my mouth to say—

Then the fire alarms go off, an air raid!

We both leap off the couch. She grabs the phone and stops the attack.

"What?" she shouts.

I know it's my son Richard. I'm furious, this is it. I can't take it any more. I'm near tears, I hold out my hand for the receiver.

"For Chrissake Roge," she yells. "It's way too late!"

I bend down to find my shoes, I should be going anyhow. I need to *think*. Maybe I'll call Mo, she'd understand even in the middle of the night. Where to call from though, a pay phone I guess. But then I'll be out even later, it'll have to wait until I'm in my office at work— with the door locked.

When Darlene hangs up the phone, I go to give her a quick hug, I think it'll be okay. I hope it's okay. *I'm too tired, I really need to talk to someone.*

I hug her. I hug her. It's a hug I've needed for six years. She holds on to me, and I hold her. I love her, even though I might not tomorrow, right now falling over with exhaustion, I know I love her as much as I've loved any lady in my whole life.

And then she looks up at me for a moment and shuts her eyes and kisses me. On the mouth. We do this for a long time. And I like it and I'm very confused.

Marsha, you stop that this minute. She's straight— got it?

You live in this town, and when she freaks out in the morning, who's going to be in trouble?

And we still keep on hugging and kissing.

I can't begin to describe how much I like kissing her.

But I'm afraid she's going to hate me for it, even though she started it.

Most of all I'm scared I'm going to hate me.

One thing's for sure, I'm not going to be accused of seducing innocent ladies. I ask her right out, "Do you want me to stay or go?"

She leads me into the bedroom; I can't seem to open my mouth to say, "Uh, no, I'm not ready to be in your bedroom yet," and then we are already lying on the bed. It's a relief to lie down though. We hold hands for a very long time, not talking. Lying next to her, I'm grateful it's so dark and she can't see my tears. I almost forget who she is, remembering the sweet times in my life I have lain next to, and loved, another female. I remember so acutely, *yes* with my body, but not *just* my body, what that felt like and how much of my life I've stopped living because I can't have that any more.

Then I realize it might be really wrong to be here, it's Darlene I'm next to now; I like her, but I don't really know her. This, here, now, might be wrong—but it's *not* wrong, what I've done in my life, who I've been, who I've loved.

Everything else is wrong though, I have to face it, everything is grossly, obscenely, horribly perverted: letting my life be ruled by a seventeen-year-old tyrant, by a sweet little boy who will 'get hormones' whether he wants them or not, and by their father! What am I doing? They're his, they've always been his. He can have them! I could go back to Chicago. . .

Marsha: 1962

Suddenly I remember I'm at Darlene's. Darlene's? I wake up:
"*What* are you doing?"
"I didn't mean—"
"I was *asleep!*"
"I, uh, I . . ."
"You didn't even ask!"
I stand up to go, then catch the shamed look on Darlene's face. Crouching down by the side of the bed, I hold my hand out to her. She puts her fingers lightly on my palm.
"Darlene, there's nothing wrong with wanting to touch another gal. Don't be thinking that."
She keeps her gaze on our hands, blinks a few times.
"Hey," I squeeze her fingers gently, "I think you're as cute as a bug in a rug, clever too. Don't be telling yourself make-believe stories."
She looks at me finally. "I really didn't mean . . . I don't want to be like Rob—"
"Ron."
"I mean Roge." She smiles.
Then I remember.
"I've made up my mind!" I stand up. "I'm going to Chicago. I'm going back!"

The Mouse-Gray Suitcase

Celia had wild gray and white hair that stuck out uncontrollably around her face, and lots of extra skin hanging down from her big upper arms.

They said she was my father's second cousin, once removed. I saw no resemblance.

I can't imagine what she made of me: a spunky fourteen-year old, in brown hiphugger bellbottoms and psychedelic shirt, the day I arrived in my father's pickup truck.

We were both stubborn, embarrassments to our families. This, we were informed separately, was our last chance before more drastic measures would be taken.

"We'd hate to have to put her in a nursing home," her family told me, listing her various crimes (or sins depending on which member was doing the complaining) in a helpless whisper.

What my family had in mind for me if this didn't stick, I wasn't planning to hang around and find out.

The suitcase sat on the front seat of the pickup between my father and me. It was the same mouse-gray suitcase that my mother had used on her many trips to the hospital over the years when she gave birth to all of my brothers, sisters, and of course, I supposed, to me. It contained a pair of faded, patched, and frayed blue jeans, one oversize green T-shirt stolen from my older brother, my art supplies, and my secret brown-paper-bag-covered copy of *The Feminine Mystique*.

My father was talking, but if he thought I was listening, he was a fool.

"And we expect you to be decent over there in town."

I was busy watching the farmhouses through the truck window as we sped past, the neighbors I'd had all my life. I would not be a country kid any more, I'd be one

The Mouse-Gray Suitcase

of *them*. It was all because of an old lady named Celia; I made a mental note to be extra nice to her.

We ate dinner in silence for the most part. Efforts to have discussions of any sort quickly frustrated both of us. I would give up after a few of her What-what-did-you-say's, feeling too shy to shout something I wasn't sure didn't sound dumb in the first place.

After dinner, I would clear the table while she stuffed the leftover beef bones into an empty milk carton, and then added them to the huge collection already packed into her freezer.

"For John's dogs," she'd explain.

"Six thirty yet?" she'd ask right after the table was cleared.

"Turn on that nice show," she'd point at the ancient set. "Lassie."

Then as soon as the show ended, she'd pull herself up and turn toward the back bedroom, questioning me: "Aren't you going to bed yet?"

"Too early," I'd shout back. "I have homework. Study."

I'd point at my books. She'd shake her head, get her bearings and amble slowly towards her room.

Once settled under her quilt she rarely got up, I knew, until the sun rose. Still, I left a window open just in case she should call out for me as I sat on the picnic table in the back yard, necking with Kim Schmidt, a girl from the junior class who lived at the end of the block.

Coming home after school, I'd find her sitting on that same picnic table, grinning wickedly, chomping down plums she'd plucked from the overhanging branches. Turning to acknowledge my presence, she would continue spitting out pit after pit with deliberate enthusiasm. I'd count thirty or forty of them at a sitting.

She took special pride in baking me treats. Once it was a strawberry pie; it must have contained nine cups of sugar to one of fruit. I barely managed to finish one polite piece when she broke the news to me.

"Now, that whole thing is yours dear," she pointed at the rest of the pie. "I can't have any sugar they say because of the diabetes."

She talked about her now grown-up grandchildren: "Oh, they come to visit about once a blue moon. Once a blue moon."

They lived right in town too, they paid me five bucks a week to stay with her. I thought it was good money.

The day I knew Celia and I weren't going to make it after all was when she got stuck in the bathtub for the third time. I wanted so badly to pull her out. I tried: grabbing on to her wet old arm with all my strength, our eyes desperate on each other, no words. I had to call her family; they came right away.

Celia cried, to be seen like that without any clothes on. They got her out, and then sat around in the kitchen talking.

"Look, no one can say we didn't give it a good shot keeping her at home," the daughter was saying to her brother. "John, she should really move in with you, now that your house is finished."

"Why don't you let her live in your goddamn house?" the brother said back real nasty.

I was standing right there. Celia, too, wrapped in her fuzzy baby blue robe. I was afraid that if I moved, they might notice me—us. We went quickly, quietly into the living room. I turned on the TV, and we settled into our chairs. It was the one where Lassie doesn't come home; Celia had tears leaking out of her eyes.

"Well, I'm turning in," she told me.

She hadn't hurt herself in the tub, just gotten stuck; I wanted to march out into that kitchen and tell them that.

Instead, I went to my room and packed my stuff into the mouse-gray suitcase.

Glad to Meet You

It was Montana she woke up to. Montana, though not the wild one of her childhood; the old house now overlooked condos instead of forest. She wondered why in the world she had come.

Her parents were talking in the kitchen; Caroline could hear every word. Arriving exhausted the previous evening, Caroline, Linda, and the kids had just crashed. Evelyn was on her night shift and didn't even get the glimpse of them that Kendall caught; and Caroline had few words for him.

In her early morning restlessness, Caroline pulled boxes from the closet. Old birthday party invitations, horse show ribbons; she couldn't believe it was all still here. Couldn't believe she hadn't destroyed every last piece of it before she had run away, a hippie teenager determined never to step foot in this house again. She made plans to throw it into the burning barrel once the day got going.

"Burning barrel!" Kendall would snort later; "They have ordinances about that stuff now. Haven't had one in ages. We've got regular garbage and everything these days."

Knowing her lover was not really asleep, Caroline leaned into Linda's back and asked, "Nervous? How are you doing?"

"You're making one hell of a lot of noise rustling that crap around, you know!" Linda snarled.

Well, she's talking, better than the big silence, Caroline supposed. *If I can just get the right tone of voice—wait—what the fuck am I doing?* Caroline pulled back abruptly: *I hate that game, tiptoeing around; I'm not her damn wife.*

Glad to Meet You

"What am I supposed to wear?" Linda hissed.

Staring out the window, Caroline remembered how she had longed to be a hawk when she was a child: to soar over the ridge. Learning to ride had come closest to it. Sitting in the saddle of a horse named Betsy Bliss, Caroline had been able to shut her eyes and make do.

Caroline looked at the sky: Montana Blue, the sun bright, tree branches moving slightly; it stirred an ancient loss. She wanted to fly right now! *Out that window with me—all that space. I'd never come back, nothing would hold me down again.*

"You don't have to have wings to fly, Girl." Grandma, in the garden, looking up from the green beans: "Just shut your eyes and take off. Do it all the time myself, child."

"I'll bet it's crisp out there," Caroline finally replied.

"I'm not talking about the weather. I mean I don't know what to *wear*. I shouldn't have come. I shouldn't be here!"

A rush of homesickness hit Caroline then: homesickness for the old house in Madison, near the zoo, before the kids were born. Just her and the garden. Montana was beautiful, she did miss it, but with a confused anger. What she missed was not here any more. Maybe never had been. Linda was right: she shouldn't be here. *They* shouldn't be here. They shouldn't be anywhere together. Heck, they shouldn't *be* together.

"Hey, you wanted to come. This was your idea, remember."

"That's because I want to give you something. What else can I do for you? The way you talk about the mountains, the horses, the air itself. I wanted to give you that."

"I wanted us to have a real family vacation," Linda said. "Then it turns out to be such a long drive, and the boys fighting so loud."

"This *is* a real family vacation. Real families fight, and anyhow it wasn't just the boys."

"Well you have to discuss every little thing. *Why* couldn't we eat at MacDonald's just one time? Why does everything have to be political? Shit, isn't this vacation?"

"Nobody said *you* couldn't eat at MacDonald's."

"But I don't want to eat by myself. I didn't get involved with you so I could be by myself."

Don't fight with her now.

"I shouldn't be here," Linda whined. "Your parents are going to know. They'll hate me for corrupting their only living child."

"Like, I really needed corrupting. I don't care what my parents think. Come out to them or don't. I've just never been close enough to go through all the drama."

"Bad enough that I'm out to mine! I'm not coming out to yours."

Resentfully, Linda watched Caroline shuffle through a box of junk, twitter on in an idiotic high voice, "Oh this ribbon! I remember that show! Duncan stepped into horse shit as the judge was handing him the trophy."

Shut up, Linda wanted to say. *Sometimes I hate her.*

Linda gave herself a pep talk: *You deal with important people every day at work. These are simple small town hicks in the middle of nowhere. What the hell are you so scared of? Get yourself together!*

"I feel sick," Linda said out loud.

"I'll show you where the bathroom is."

The boys turned over in their sleeping bags at that moment: "Hey, we're at Grandpa's and Grandma's!"

Linda froze. Caroline's parents couldn't have missed that.

"Grandpa and Grandma's, finally!" Skye jumped off the floor.

Caroline stopped them from charging out of the room in their pajamas.

"Clothes first." She handed each boy a fresh pair of jeans, underwear, and a shirt. "Socks too, guys."

Dressed, the boys tore out of the room. A few seconds later, Caroline and Linda heard their voices loudly rising from the kitchen.

Glad to Meet You

"Well, look who's here!" Grandma was saying.

"Couple of sleepyheads! You finally decided to join us, huh? Well, aren't you a couple of rascals. Aren't they big, Ev? Didn't I tell you? She didn't want to believe me. Well, aren't they?" Grandpa was hollering.

"How would you guys like some pancakes?"

"I've got to go join them, Linda. My parents will wonder where I am. What's taking me so long." Caroline ran a brush through her hair, put her earrings in.

"Go!" Linda pulled the blanket up to her ears and squeezed her eyes shut.

"If you don't get up soon they're going to think you're real weird."

"Oh, that's supportive of you."

"Okay, what do you want me to do? Come with me and get it over with. Think of it as an adventure."

No response.

The pancakes were piled high on the kitchen table. Caroline hadn't noticed last night that the cabinets had been painted an orange enamel, matched by new curtains in a pattern of brilliant orange and buttercup butterflies. For a second, Caroline tried to imagine Linda's mother standing in this kitchen. The enamel would definitely clash with Vivian's designer fingernails.

"How you doing, Ma?"

Evelyn handed Caroline a plate of pancakes.

"Well, Caroline, look at you! My goodness, you look good. You really are getting older. We all are I guess! My goodness, are those really grays in your hair? Shame on you, you should use a little something for that.

"I saw that old horse-riding buddy of yours, Molly, last week at the market, and she looked a million bucks. She has her hair all permed nice. She even gets her nails done! Can you imagine? In a town like this. She could have been a model, really, she could have. You both were such a cute couple of girls. You should look her up. You look good Caroline, really you do."

By the time Caroline finished her pancakes she was exhausted. Her mother had always ignored her before the boys were born; now she finally found some value in her daughter.

"Well, we are so excited! Pa had to practically hold me back from waking you right up last night after I got in from my shift. Look how big my boys have gotten!" Evelyn gave each of the boys another pancake. They ate them.

"And where is that nice girl who drove with you? You always did have one good chum. That Molly, I saw her last week— did I say? Tell that girlfriend to come on down. She's not shy, is she?"

Caroline could feel the words seeping through the ceiling. "She sleeps late Ma. She's a city girl, you know."

"Well! We practically live in town ourselves now with all the building and what-not going on around here. You wouldn't recognize the place."

Skye was dragging his fingers through the maple syrup left on his plate, happily licking them off. His older brother sat and stared at Grandpa, who was grunting his agreement with Grandma.

"Excuse me, I'll be back in a sec." Caroline spoke over her shoulder as she headed for the stairs.

Upstairs, Linda was still in bed facing the wall.

The boys were playing out in the front yard when Caroline returned to the kitchen again— alone. The door opened and Ev scurried in.

"And did you notice?" Ev pointed at the cabinets of the remodeled kitchen.

"Oh, did you do this recently? It's . . . it's very orange, Ma. Extremely!" Caroline hoped she sounded positive.

"Oh you! You never liked bright colors! It's cheerful," said Ev, wiping her hands on a yellow dish towel. "Has that girl ever been to Montana before?"

"First time."

"Well then, you have to take her to see some of our beautiful scenery. Take her camping. Show her the ghost towns, she *has* to see the ghost towns."

Glad to Meet You

"We camped all the way out here, Ma!"

"You can't do too much with boys. They're at the right age for it. Do them some good, considering."

Caroline passed up the bait, and excused herself. Again.

"Linda, please get up. I'll help you find something to wear, if you like."

"There's no way I won't look like a dyke," said Linda from under the covers.

"Oh, for Pete's sake, your own goddamn parents didn't notice for years. *My parents are not going to know you're a dyke!*" Caroline caught herself, and glanced at the floor. "Look, of course you look like a dyke," she said softly. "That's one of the reasons I'm attracted to you."

Linda didn't budge.

"I give up! That's it. It's not going to get any easier!" Caroline stomped out of the room. "People in the country *do not* stay in bed all day."

Ev was cleaning up the breakfast mess and humming when Caroline returned. Why the hell were mothers always cleaning something? Why couldn't they sit down and talk for a change? And Kendall had never lifted one hand to help with any of this. Caroline grabbed a towel and began to dry.

"Now I hope you like what I'm planning for dinner. I got it special for you. Are you still so darn fussy about what you eat? It was terrible last time not to let the boys eat that good steak. Boys need meat. They need it for their bones. I work in a hospital, I know."

Caroline silently concentrated on putting a deep shine on each of the plates.

"I hope your friend doesn't mind the accommodations." Ev asked.

As if this were the Holiday Inn, or something.

"I figured the boys would get by fine in their sleeping bags. You girls don't mind sharing that big old bed do you?"

I will not scream. No mother, why would we mind it here any more than we do every night at home?

Suddenly, in walked a handsome butch.

She appeared like magic. Out of nowhere. Her short blond hair slicked back close against her head, dark tailored pants, tight at the ankles, shiny pointy-toed boots— and that shirt! Where in the world had Linda found that western pearl-button shirt?

Caroline openly stared at her lover: *women's shirt, women's pants* —

"Mom, this is my friend," she finally choked out. "Linda."

What is that making her hair so dark, grease? Oh, the shower.

Linda was shaking Ev's hand vigorously, saying in a voice abnormally deep with nervousness, "Glad to make your acquaintance, Ev. Glad to meet you."

The Big Blue Ford

A big blue car pulls into our driveway.
My brother says, "That's a Ford!"
"You don't know."
"You better go out and get mom," he says.
"Don't you boss me, I'm bigger!"
As the car pulls up next to us, my brother holds back the dog—the dog won't bite you, but nobody ever believes it when he's barking like that.

I run fast as I can down to the tomato patch behind the shed. The noise of the tiller gets closer, and I spot my mother out there pushing the big machine between long rows and rows of tomatoes. The soil is so hard and hot beneath my feet, I have to hop-run across it.

"Mommy!" I shout.

She can't hear me 'cause that thing is so loud. I get close to touch her freckled arm.

"Mommy!" I yell again.

"What?!" she answers. She doesn't like to be disturbed when she's out here.

"I got work to do," she usually says, "this field has got to be tilled before it rains—and it's gonna rain soon, bugs are out. Who's gonnna do it, if I don't? Then what are we gonna eat all winter?"

Usually she says, "Don't be pestering me."

"Mommy, somebody's here."

I can smell her skin, the sweat mixed with tomato together with the gas-smoke from the tiller.

"Who is it?"

"I don't know, somebody in a new blue Ford."

My mom stops the tiller.

"Oh my Good Lord, how can they come at a time like this? Look at me! I'm gonna die."

The Big Blue Ford

My mother hurries back up to the driveway; I trot along beside her. She talks nervously the whole way: "What do they expect farmers to be doing in the middle of a summer day? Just sitting around waiting for some big shot to come calling? What I'm wearing—I haven't even got a bra on."

She tries to fix her hair with her fingers.

I'm looking at her; she's wearing an old orange and brown sleeveless shirt, shorts that come down to her knees, dust-covered boots, gray anklets (I guess they used to be white). She looks like she always does, normal.

She's walking faster now, and still talking. I know better than to open my mouth.

"My God! And look at you kids—filthy, every one of you! And where'd you get all those scratches on your legs? I told you not to play in the oat bin. I bet the house is a pigpen—you'd better run ahead and sweep up a little."

I do as she asks, but it's not much more than five minutes before I see them through the window heading towards the house. The little kids are hanging all over Mom. All the bigger kids are out in the field haying.

"Let me just get you a cup of coffee—" my mom is offering as the two enter the room.

"Don't need any coffee. Thank you," the woman says.

My mother glares at me as though I am doing something wrong just by standing there.

I've never seen this lady before. She's not one of my relatives, that's for sure. This lady is a city lady. She has the most beautiful shoes in the world, with a purse that matches, all made out of some brown crinkly stuff. Her nylons don't even have one run in them, and her dress is nicer than anything I've seen even in church.

I figure she must be very kind because she is dressed special like a queen. When I look into her face I'm startled by her stare, directed right at me; it's a sharp poke in the stomach.

I go back into the kitchen. Maybe that lady doesn't like my bare feet, I think. I look at the dirty summer calluses I've built up. Maybe she doesn't know how tough my feet are, that I'm careful not to step on rusty nails.

I go into the bathroom and crawl up onto the sink so I can see myself in the mirror. Two big brown eyes look back at me. Maybe the lady would like me if I brushed my hair.

The noise of the little kids draws me back to the kitchen; my mom wouldn't like them inside: "You get back outside. Go play in the sandbox."

"You can't boss!" they say.

But I really am bigger, and they go.

Then I lean against the kitchen wall, and listen to the conversation from the dining room.

"What I fail to understand is why you would even want to take that girl in when you've got ten children of your own to feed and support already. Judging by the income reports. . ." the lady is saying.

The smell of the lady's cigarette fills our house. She talks to my mom in the same voice the nuns use when they are acting nice, but I know what they're really doing is checking all the black spots where my sheet-white soul is supposed to be.

I can barely hear my mom's response 'cause she's mumbling. This is my mom who can yell all the way across the farm at one of us kids when she's mad.

I want to tell her, "Speak up."

"That child is my niece. Can't a family take care of its own? Would you want one of your relations to go and live at some stranger's house? What is one more child gonna hurt me?"

I know what's going on, I hear the big kids talk. My cousin, the one who doesn't live on a farm like us, her mother is dying.

"They live in a shack down by the river," my mom told me once. "With a potty right in the middle of the room."

I tried to figure out how you would pee with everyone looking at you.

My cousin is older than me. We played one time when her mom first got sick. The big kids say her mom is going to die, 'cause her skin got green and she can't

The Big Blue Ford

breathe. I heard my mom say she doesn't have any meat on her bones 'cause she smoked too many cigarettes.

"That girl's father is my own brother. I know he can't take care of any little girl. He's not right in the head, he got too many shock treatments after the war."

The smoke makes my eyes sting as it drifts out.

I would like my cousin to come and live here. We need more girls.

The visiting lady is making noises with her papers. I hear her push back the chair along the wooden floor.

Quickly, I move over to the sink and pull up a chair to stand on so I look like I'm doing the dishes.

My mom comes walking past me with the lady. They go out, and I watch through the window. My mom offers the lady her hand to shake, but the lady is already in her car and doesn't notice.

My mom comes back into the house with all the little kids following her. She sits on a chair, she doesn't say anything, just keeps watching us all.

Finally she says to me, "You make these kids some Kool Aid. It's awfully hot."

She goes into the bedroom and comes back out with a package of the stuff she's got stashed somewhere. She's got her Sunday purse and chapel veil in its little plastic container, and the truck keys in her hand.

"Drink your Kool Aid. I'll be back in a bit."

I don't know why she gave us Kool Aid.

She didn't say where she was going, but I could see her as clearly as if she had taken me along. She'd pull her truck up into the big parking lot. It'd be the only one there, middle of the week, unless there was a funeral which there wasn't today. She'd go into that old Church, through the heavy doors where you walk under the big bell. She would march right down to the first row, and sit down. It'd be all quiet and cool and dark in there. She'd look at the pictures, especially the one with Mary. She'd close her eyes all scrunchy like a witch or something making a spell. If I were with her, she would make me play outside, while she sat. And I would like that 'cause all those pictures and stuff make me feel creepy.

When she came out I would ask, "What did you do in there all by yourself?"

She would tell me, "We gotta ask for rain."

Or, "Your brother's gotta get well."

Or, "Those baby chicks gotta make it through these first few days."

If I asked her this time, she'd say, "That cousin of yours has gotta have a home."

As I cleaned up the Kool Aid cups I felt settled. Through the window, I saw the truck pulling into the driveway. My mother gave her purse and stuff to one of the little kids to bring into the house.

I watched her as she walked back down to the tomato patch.

"Who's gonna do it, if I don't?" she would say if anyone tried to stop her.

My Mother
Played the Accordion

It is the smell, the open gray metal accordion case, it floats out like a ghost. My mother stands in the Good Room laughing again like a girl, the music strapped to her chest, part of her broad shoulders. She plays; I dance a child's polka. I press my cheek against the crimson velvet lining, run the backs of my arms along the smooth buttons, the colored inlays.

A luxury, this memory: our private life.

Only once he walked in, the last time.

"Oh for Christ's sake Vera, not that again. You don't have enough to do without making a commotion too."

i arrived a fool with my seventeen years and hope my grandmothers accordion wedding gift three sticks vine charcoal one pad paper from nuns five year diary four lines per day expecting by eighteen

Is this how it was for her: he is in the kitchen where I am washing the dishes. He never takes his eyes from my back, stays in his chair and doesn't move to help but doesn't shut up for telling me how each plate should be rinsed thoroughly as I am doing just that, how the baby bottles must be scrubbed with the bottle brush which I am already holding in my hand. Why do I go around so dumpy all the time he wants to know, put on such an act, and don't I know how lucky I am.

I despise my own face when tears are stronger than my pride. I turn and face him, "Get out of here. Get!"

He charges, grabs me . . .

"It will happen to me, I am becoming her. You are making me into her. Leave me alone!"

He is purple, ripping my shirt, screaming into my face, "You little bitch, don't you dare say I had anything to do with it, she was nuts, crazy, a mental case from the word go—you got that, you got that!"

My Mother Played the Accordion

I smash his head with the soapy plate still dripping in my hand, it breaks against his crown. I hit him again, he bleeds, stares, stunned a moment out of his attack.

"You," I say, with absolute certainty, "you—are an assassin."

And then I run, I run out of the house, down the highway. I run and run wondering where can I go, finally dropping into a ditch where I wipe the sweat from my eyes with the dishcloth, and make a plan.

beautiful babies yes i want to crawl into a hole in the ground awake every night his rage make the infant stop nothing consoles what is wrong what power do i have

no he says i dont have good christian love any more im not nice im not im chipped at chipped away

i am starving to death there is a cavern in my chest my life seeping out

For five years I lived in an apartment down the street from a place called Misty Manor. Twice a day the patients were paraded past my bedroom window: arms hanging stiffly, heads loose atop curled-in shoulders, sluggish robotic steps. Prisoners of war: daily I was reminded what it was my mother escaped.

i dreamed i was walking many other people were walking yet i am alone thinking how the bomb could drop wouldnt that be justice after all i have waited so long to die that doesnt mean that i want the whole world to disappear that doesnt mean somewhere for me for the future for not just my children i have hope it is not enough

in the dream i came upon a friend she was like me locked in sitting unclothed as they make us times they think we will try anything she was weeping i said come on it is time to continue

the path was narrow water on one side but deep the other razor rocks no choice but i did attempt the rocks regardless pulled down by attendant i knocked him away but did not escape

a woman with an infant whispered to me you will come to a place tell them you want to sleep not shower
i see already the barns i hear the showers
i want to sleep the man does not understand he takes me into a room where all the men sit around a table they speak to one another but my language no one can comprehend

Once in the attic I found four yellowed charcoal drawings of an infant sleeping in a wooden cradle. It was dated the year of my birth, no signature. I have searched and never come across them again.

Once I was walking down the basement steps and came upon these words scrawled in a child's hand with charcoal: why is mom playing with death. Perhaps it was a dream.

depressed is the word he said shame on you a pretty girl get over that nonsense
i write here even when it betrays me
the thought of any more need of even words i am so afraid of losing more than i have what do i have ever will have a woman only has her secrets

She is standing in the kitchen, much taller than me. I am the invisible witness to her howling deathwish, terrified to leave her alone. I don't know where to hide or how I can save her. I am Alice getting smaller by the minute.

they say this will pass truth is it will return again too

Once not so long ago she cradled me, told me I was magic, made her ring sparkle in the light shining through the ice on the window: "See."

If they say she was a monster they don't know.

Under my feather quilt I am safe, angry, I want to know why her, who I love, and not him, who deserves it. I want to know.

My Mother Played the Accordion

things i want to be true i dont write down when have i ever not had a face reading over my shoulder cut it out rip it out that is what they cant bear that a woman should have her secrets

My father is driving the car too fast down a steep hill.

My mother is coming back to us, they have let her out after three years. She sits pale, in a mint-green pantsuit, fragile, her hair sprayed stiff with Final Net.

am i so terrible
i dont want to see gawking up at me from the page dont i know enough to not say more if i got drunk i would tell stories until they set me on fire
so who cares so i dont so who wants to read it anyway

They think her love for me is stronger than her will to escape. I do my part by never once taking my eyes off her. I don't know what they see; I see my mother.

She has the knife in her hand, she is fast, suddenly strong, she breaks for the bathroom, with a quick hand she locks me out. Let me in, let me.

how exposed one feels suddenly when the blood really does come out
runs on the sink wounds really running from my arm see i am real i am a painter, carver
if i act quickly no one will know no one will know no one

I run for rescue in slow motion crying, I betray her; I am no different. Backing away from the grip of two strong men, she turns, pushes me onto the floor in her rage.

Her rage, her life; I want her life so much. I do not think I can survive without it.

From then on we share no secrets. From then on I listen to her tortured sounds, vomiting the overdoses, his fingers down her throat. I can be no comfort, find none for myself.

there is one thing they can not make me do that is live not even if they outsmart my body
this prison is a prison is my home where i wait cant move unless he springs the trap
dont they know i am not for waiting

My father was beating me with his fists, I felt I would die. I looked up and saw her sitting, alive again: silent, pale, observing. I realized it was a dream, she spoke to him through me, "I will destroy you, don't doubt it."

i walk down the street stare go ahead a curiosity i look into a store window that reflection is not me
what is it they want i fix my eyes straight ahead look only direct or meet their eyes with nothing in mine a skill i have pull my mind to a safe world
there is no safe place to go crazy what i didnt know there is no cure it only gets worse the drugs take away they cut it doesnt end doesnt heal it doesnt there is only one end to this path
once i was blue it was mine now i have nothing not my own body not pride dont push away they say i trust no one
spare me your pity

"You say you are weeping about the woman found strangled at the edge of campus, but really that's an excuse for deeper grief. Don't put your problems on the world."
Out of superstition and mother-loyalty, I avoided the doctors who gave pills, did surgery. A therapist instead: eighty dollars a fix. As I came down each time that voice haunted me, "No of course you're not queer. You hate your father, but not all men are like him."
Out of rage, common sense, I dismissed the dealers, learned to dismantle my own bombs and return them carefully to their origin: reset.

My Mother Played the Accordion

> there is no pill to make him stop
> no operation to cut away time for me no hospital to give me peace of mind time to hold the baby all night there is no cure
> the gold stars mean nothing to me i wont work for them im sick to not want gold gummy stars alright im sick
> he said not the time for questions not the time to think

I think of my mother's act of rebellion: she wouldn't live for them.

I think of my own and know: I won't die for them.

> it is not because i dont love my life it is because i love it very much

I don't know what they see; I see my mother. No one tucked away hankies that day and said, "But what an accurate portrait Vera could draw, a born artist she was."

No one recalled, "Vera played a fine tune, that you could count on. That you could remember."

Maybe I was too young to know. After all no one really is a born artist. More than inclination it takes hours, money, and for a woman a voice in her own time that reminds her, "It is right to want to do this above all else."

> it is not because i dont love my life it is because i love it very much

I hear the hushed gossip of cowards behind me in the grocery store, asking about my mother: what did she do, what did she do, what did she do. They don't hear. It is only a whisper:

> My mother played the accordion. That is what she did.

Wishing on White Horses

1.

"No, wait with that rocking horse. I want to tie that to the very top," Jupe shouts across the truck to Caroline.
"All right, all right. Pull that horse off."
"Be careful with those skis."

Where have they been so long, friends? Then Caroline remembers.
"What do you want to hang out with Donna for, she's a separatist."
"Jupe doesn't like me."
"You never have enough time for me, how come you can find time for Pam?"

"This is like open-heart surgery."
Donna pats Caroline's shoulder, then checks the truckbed to find the perfect spot to squeeze in one more box.
"Guess I'm not very funny any more." Caroline helps to hoist the crate of books into place.
"Heartbreak isn't all that amusing of a subject."
"It does get old fast," Caroline says. "Just the petty details change."
"Where do you want this mirror?" Jupe interrupts.
"I don't care."
"Don't want it to bust."
"Look, I don't care about it. In fact, Jupe, if you want that mirror, it's yours. Belonged to some old housemate, it distorts horribly."

Wishing on White Horses

"It's watching you kill yourself. As long as you stay with Linda, I can't be around you."

"Tuck it in here behind the dresser."
"Let's wrap it in this towel then."

Why does it take so long? We've got to get this stuff out of here before five, five, five, Linda will be home at five.

"Yours or Linda's?" Pam holds up the shamrock.
"Mine. That plant blooms for my birthday every year. I've had it since before Skye; in fact, I gave birth under the windowsill, looking up at that plant."
"So, I guess you want it huh."

Mine, what is mine.
My children. Her dog. Her cat. Her house.

"Don't pack the plant, I'll take it in my car."
"She's going to be pissed when she comes home."
"Fuck her," Jupe says.

The boxes finally loaded, Donna and Pam drive off in the packed funky truck. Jupe leaves for work.

Caroline enters Linda's house for a final check; she crosses the living room, the polished wooden floor . . . recalls sanding these floors with Linda. Sanding by hand, and rented machine. Sanding between the coats of varnish, and late at night after the boys were asleep. It was good working together, telling stories; Caroline was impressed with her lover's strength and confidence about how best to approach each step in the process. Every corner, meticulous, a hassle, but gorgeous now. Linda will probably cover them with oriental rugs with the boys gone.

The white walls of the living room:
"I want you to help me choose." Linda, at Ace Hardware.
"Um, I don't know."
"It's our house. I want you to choose with me."
"Let's look at the samples," Caroline had suggested. Our house, but Linda's credit card.
"How about this?" Linda had held up a sample.
"White?"
"Eggshell. Do you like it?"
"It's fine."
"I don't want it to be 'fine'! I want eggshell, and I want you to want eggshell too. Do you want eggshell!"

Caroline walks up the stairs to the bedroom. The tall bureau with its elegant framed mirror reflects the bed. Caroline runs her hand across the smooth, deep-grained, carved inlays of the heirloom, the rich contrast of blond and mahogany, the centerpiece: this narrow bed. It has always puzzled Caroline: the sheer magnificence of the object, yet a foam futon on the floor gives a more restful night's sleep.

She leans against the wall, overwhelmed for a moment by the jumble of memories: the hours spent making love here, the night terrors Linda comforted here, and recently more than anything else, the bitter tension, the fights, with Linda's threats and the apologies that followed.

The closet is still full, it's weird considering how much Caroline has taken out. On the floor are 501's, Adidas and sweats mingled with old nylons. The fine wool suits, the narrow skirts . . . mornings Caroline, still in bed, watched sleepily as Linda sucked in her stomach to get the zipper up in the back. Those pale linen summer suits, the silk shirts, the high heels lined up—that costume was a fleeting, early-rising Linda to whom Caroline never adjusted.

Caroline closes the closet.
Linda is driving home from work right now.

Wishing on White Horses

Usually Linda likes commuting; it gives her time to fantasize. She turns up the car stereo, drives comfortably in stocking feet. She forgets the tight suit and the blouse with its damn clown's bow irritating her chin. Listening to Cris Williamson, she watches the rolling hills and the farmers' fields changing throughout the year, all the while keeping an eye out for white horses.

Once when Caroline drove this route with Linda on the way to Milwaukee, Linda burst out, "Look, Caroline!" and pointed at the two milky horses munching grass in the meadow off the freeway.

"Oh! They're spectacular," Caroline had exclaimed.

"White horses are for wishes," Linda had explained. "Every day on my way to work when I see those horses I make the same wish: 'Make Caroline mine forever. Make Caroline mine, and I swear I'll never ask for anything else.' "

And Linda really did make that wish.

Caroline had looked uncomfortable for a moment, Linda hadn't understood why. Then Caroline had said, "I never heard of that before."

"Sandy and I did it in high school. When you see a white horse—quick spit in your palm and trace an X into it, then make your wish," Linda had told her.

Today Linda hates the drive, it forces her to think. No amount of fussing with cassettes, or elaborate ideas, can combat the persistent memory of the previous night. It plays itself over and over in her brain:

"What, and I don't get any say? That's not fair. I've had to work all week and this is the first time in a month we have a weekend without the boys. I have a right to some time with my lover, damn it."

"Can't you understand, I'm going out of my mind! I need time to figure things out."

"I'll be playing volleyball all Saturday afternoon, and tennis on Sunday morning. That'll give you time."

"This isn't up for discussion."

"And how come you wouldn't go camping with me? Huh? And don't you look at me like that, that was a whole month ago and anyway you pushed me over the edge. You just won't drop it. I'm not going to put up with this crap. Stop running away, Caroline. What in the hell are you going to figure out about our relationship without me being there?"

Caroline had got up from the couch and walked across the room.

"Don't walk out on me. Talk to me. Talk to me!"

"I'm going to take a bath."

Linda had grabbed Caroline's arm and pulled her lover back. "We're getting worse and worse. You're stressed out—it's not me, it's the boys and school you need a break from."

"Cynthia is taking the boys for the next month, maybe longer."

"Gee thanks for telling me!"

"I only found out today. Look we'll talk later, I'm too depressed, I can't think right now."

"You're going to leave me." Linda had tightened her hold on Caroline's upper arm. "I can tell."

"Hey! That hurts." Caroline had tried to pull her arm out from Linda's grip and snapped, "Let me go!"

"No, you're going to talk to me, goddamn it, Talk to Me! If you're going to leave tell me now. I'm not going to be sitting around churning all weekend. You tell me," Linda had demanded. "Damn it! I'm not waiting the way I did for Sandy like a fool while she drove me nuts. If you go away this weekend we're through."

"I'm going." Caroline instinctively curled her shoulders in and put her hand over her stomach.

Driving past the horses today, Linda is filled suddenly with rage and yells right out the window:

"FUCK white horses! You assholes!"

She wants to swerve her new car off the freeway, ram right through them. How dare they stand out in that field still looking perfect? How dare they not keep up their end of the bargain? Those white horses are fuckers!

Wishing on White Horses

"Look what we've got. I go to work every day, those people talk about their nice houses, kids, pets, life at home, and I just smile to myself. I've got all that too. Sure, we've got problems just like everyone else. So what? It's the American Dream, Caroline, just one better."

"The perfect little marriage." Caroline had turned and yanked her arm free. "Shit, I never wanted that even when I was straight."

Caroline closes the bedroom door behind her; she doesn't open the one to the boys' room at all, she knows for certain it's empty.

In the gray-blue bathroom, she sits on the edge of the claw-foot tub. She wants to have a bath now, how it would soothe her. It was pleasant the first time Linda brought her a cup of steaming cocoa to sip while she soaked. To lie in a tub that was long enough to stretch out in and read, with plenty of hot water for refills. Or to shut off the lights and be able to watch out the window the city lights over the lake, or just listen to the pelting rain, and even hail one hot August evening. To step onto the plush floor rug after, and wrap herself in the large soft pink towel.

Was it wrong to love the luxuries? Were they the reason I stayed?

Caroline touches the metal frame around the photo of a whale leaping for air; it hangs by the oval mirror against the wall. Then she opens the drawers below one by one to see if anything has been left behind. No: Linda's lipsticks, razors, hair gels, foundations, mascara, rouge . . . it still pains Caroline to see them, "Christ, Linda, how can you?"

"I had to take lessons to figure out how to put the stuff on. My mother paid, she was thrilled. It's part of the game honey, it's just a game."

Some mornings Caroline found messages scrawled across the mirror in Plum or Apple or Dusty Rose: "See you after Rugby, XXXXXXX" or "Linda X Caroline 4 Ever".

A butch in femme drag. Caroline pushes the drawer back.

LIZARDS/LOS PADRES

In the upstairs hall, at the landing above the steps, Caroline automatically turns away from the spot, then makes herself turn back and look. Nothing? She looks closely at the wall: just a tiny, barely visible break in the plaster. She touches the tender spot under her hair, then her throat and her ribs. It's nothing anyone would ever find unless they were searching. Even enraged, Linda knew better than to leave evidence.

Caroline rests on the top stair; her head aches.

The cars, bumper to bumper, have stopped. Linda rests her chin against the steering wheel before reaching over to change the tape.

She'll explain it all to Caroline tonight if she ever gets out of this traffic mess. It was just a rotten day all around, yesterday. Linda imagines taking Caroline in her arms, pulling her down across the bed and forcing her to see: *I'm sorry. It was wrong, but you wouldn't talk to me. My frustration level had been exceeded. You should have talked to me, I needed someone to talk to. It was a such a bad day, no one else understands. Work was terrible, and then Lily brought all this candy, I ate a ton of it. I even threw up. I felt like I was going crazy all afternoon, I think the sugar just got to me. Did you know my period started last night after you went to bed? I love you and I'm embarrassed, and I don't care if you want to go away this weekend. Go with my blessings, and when you come back it'll be like a new beginning.*

If only Caroline wouldn't throw that word *violence* around like she did that time when they were camping. *It isn't like I even really laid a hand on her that time.*

The car behind Linda beeps; she sees that the jam is untangling, and starts for home with new hope.

Caroline feels exhausted. Her friends responded quickly when she called them early this morning, even without knowing the details. They seemed relieved, eager to help.

It wasn't the first time Linda had acted like that. Just the first time it turned out to be more than threats.

Wishing on White Horses

I should have left last month after the camping trip. Where was I going to go with the boys? But Cynthia would gladly have taken them—I wasn't ready.
What were we even fighting about?

"Pam's going to be gone every other weekend, she's offered her place."
"What the hell are you talking about?" Linda demanded, "You can't go away every other weekend!"
"I want time for myself."
"I give you time," Linda had insisted. "Look, let's compromise. I'm willing to let you go all day Saturday and even one night a month if Pam's not going to be there."
From there it had escalated so quickly; Caroline had been shocked when Linda had pushed her up against a fallen tree: "I'm going to hit you! Damn you, I really am going to."
Linda with her fist balled up, ready. Those hard muscles, swimming muscles, weight-lifting muscles, softball muscles, those muscles that Caroline had admired . . . I'm going to smash you!"
She had calmed Linda down with reassuring words, with a quiet voice, walking with her to a spot in the woods where the water was shallow enough for wading. And when the threat seemed over she had become so numb. . .
She had sat on a large gray boulder, midstream. A tiny patch of sunlight had snuck though the branches guarding overhead and tried to pry open Caroline's eyes.
Linda had been loose then, joking, relaxed as though the threat hadn't occurred or had released the tension between them. "Come into the water with me."
Peering up at Caroline perched on the rock, Linda had tensed again and said almost desperately, "Come into the water."
When Caroline finally responded, she didn't know why she told Linda at that moment, "I dreamt about my father again last night."
Linda had moved closer, speaking quietly, approaching a wild animal with a net. "Again?"

"It's that one where he's pounding on one side of my bedroom door, and I am trying to pull the lock shut, pushing all my weight against the wood to keep him out."

Reaching up slowly then, Linda had put a palm on Caroline's shoulder. When Caroline didn't shrug it off, Linda had whispered, wanting it to be a promise, "You know I'd never <u>really</u> hit you."

Then Linda had wrapped her arms firmly around Caroline as though comforting a confused child.

Linda wanted Caroline to trust that she would be held tight. That Caroline needn't fear they would tumble off into the water. Caroline had let her do it, despising herself. Linda had kissed Caroline, that kiss with all its familiarity, its certainty.

'I am a lesbian. I'm sitting on a rock in the sun,' Caroline had thought. 'This is who I am. We are kissing.' Then horrified, she wondered, 'Why I am choosing to do this?'

Caroline stopped, jerked her body away from Linda.

'Why am I choosing to do this?'

In fact the numbness never went away. This last week Caroline skipped school one day and drove off into the country just to be out of the house, intending to make a plan.

She sat in her parked car on a gravel pullout overlooking the hills.

Hills don't have fog like mountains where the top disappears off into the sky, and a woman just has to be patient to see it come back into sight again.

Sometimes fog helps; if there was fog, I might be able to cry. But there isn't any.

Is it true, what Linda always says, that I don't trust anyone?

No. There's a good reason not to trust Linda.

Then why not leave?

I'm scared to go. I'm scared to stay.

"I'm scared as hell either way." Caroline spoke out loud. She watched the fog her words formed. She wanted to walk into the hills, but it was fall and the echo of gunshot in the distance kept her behind the glass.

Okay, Caroline thinks, as she gets up from the step, *but I am leaving now. I am choosing to leave now.*

Caroline descends the stairs, eager to be done. She goes into the kitchen, drawn to the sink, pauses to look through the elegant Victorian windows. Standing here washing the dishes, she was alone to observe the changing seasons taking place in the large backyard: the growth of blossoms into tiny sweet apples, the songbirds feeding, the amusement of the calico cat roughly playing with flies, and the cocker spaniel's struggle not to get trapped in the deep snow. Caroline opens the pantry door; Shane comes running.

"Hey, Shane." Caroline messes up the dog's ears and roughs up his wavy fur, "Yeah, yeah, how come you're so stupid? Hmmm? Yeah, you don't care what I say huh? What a furbrain. I'm gonna miss you pup. Not your fleas though or your damn hair on everything I own."

Beneath the apple tree, Caroline scoops up the cat: "I want you to come with me."

The cat narrows her eyes at Caroline.

"I know, but you belong to Linda." She brushes her ear and neck across the orange, black, and brown patches on the cat's back. "You'd be better off if you weren't so darn smart."

She carries the cat with her to the garden, and whispers to it, "And don't you dig in there this year. Do you hear?"

Linda spots some chestnut ones off to her left; of course they don't count for wishes, but still they're so powerful just standing and grazing. Linda wishes she could pull off at the next exit and go back to look at them. *Now they're true athletes, graceful and muscled.* If Caroline were in the passenger seat next to her right now they could stop, and Caroline would be so grateful, surprised even, by the gesture.

When the horses are out of sight, Linda reminds herself that it's Caroline who's always loved horses, who melted Linda with stories.

Is it so horrible? To love a woman for the life she's led, for the stories she tells?

"Just the smell made me happy, brushing them down after a day of riding on the ridge, the sweat so strong." Caroline had grinned, reminiscing.

And me at her feet soaking it in. I never really cared so much what it was that Caroline was saying, I just wanted to be near, with her. I made the mistake of telling her that once; she sulked and stopped talking. Was it wrong to want to hear that accent, to love the way she wound in and out of tales?

"When I got home from an afternoon of riding, I'd be sent to bathe. Pulling off my sweatshirt I'd be overwhelmed by the way I smelled like the horses . . . Well, I'd never have washed it off if it were up to me," Caroline had said.

Linda forces herself to concentrate on the road. In ten minutes she'll be home. She wants to be home right now. It's important to get to Caroline as soon as possible. *I should have called her. But she told me to stop calling her from work. I should have picked up some roses.*

Standing in the garden Caroline flashes on the dream she had last night.

I didn't understand who the woman was at first.

Long wiry hair, she was old and walked ahead on the path. I did a fast stride and caught up.

"So you managed to put your funeral off a week?" *I remarked calmly, as we strode along together.*

But this woman certainly was still alive.

"I want to tell you, while I still have the chance." *I felt shy,* "That is, you've meant a lot to me."

We continued walking.

"Then why did you never consider me? Why did you never care for me as much as you did your lovers?"

Perhaps the old woman hadn't meant to say 'lovers'.

"Oh, but I did."

> We embraced. I began to weep; I had wanted to for a long time.
> There was only one place this led; the woman would be buried.
> I wanted to hold the woman, hold her back.
> Perhaps it was not a church at all beyond Linda's garden. My vision was blurry. I thought it might be a church; plenty of people appeared, gathered.
> "Why can't we put off the funeral again?" I asked, desperate.
> "It's expected, Girl."
> Then the woman walked right into the arms of the funeral officials. I felt as though I was marching with her, as though we were fused, yet I didn't move forward at all.
> The old woman stood, she spoke quite plainly: "Take me, I'm ready. Go ahead."
> It was an enormous pale blue coffin that waited. The woman climbed in; I split in two: climbed in also, and at the same time, watched from a distance, myself climbing in.
> I rocked, trying to find comfort for that rising, already unbearable, grief.
> She will be buried alive behind the roses.
> "Be buried then. Make peace with it." I spoke aloud. "I'll take care of myself."
> I rocked myself awake, still weeping.

Glancing first at the roses that grow along the back fence, then at her watch, Caroline turns quickly. *Four-forty-five. I've got to get out of here.*

Caroline passes through the garage; voices come back to her:

"But the whole house is yours," Linda had insisted.

"I need some tiny place where I can be by myself," Caroline had said before moving in.

Linda had sighed, "I'll make you one in the garage if you move in. If that's what it takes."

Caroline peers up at the loft, the crude ladder. It's dark and very cold in here. The boys finally made those unfinished rafters into a hide-out, and no more was said.

Locking the garage door behind her, Caroline walks away to her car.

2.

The mechanic looks up from Caroline's old car. She asks, "You have enemies or something?"

"What?"

"First I fix that slashed back tire the other day. Now look at these spark plugs—"

"What is it?"

"There's no way this happened on its own. Someone took a pliers to 'em."

Caroline stands, feels sick. "Neighborhood boys, 'hey let's have some fun'."

The mechanic shakes her head skeptically. "Sure."

Linda keeps phoning.

On Sunday it's, "What about as friends?"

And Tuesday, "You can't cut me off from the boys like that. I'm entitled to see them."

Wednesday and Thursday, "I want to bring your stuff back, you left some things here."

"You forgot to leave the key."

Caroline tries to stay close to home, still she runs into shocked Stacy at the laundry: "I've always thought of you as the ideal couple—you could be in a Katherine Forrest book."

And cashing her check: "Why did the two of you break up, you made such a cute couple," a gay acquaintance in the Credit Union line asks.

Caroline, tired of covering up, tells him. "Not her!" he says, raising his eyebrows. "She couldn't be a *batterer*. She worked so hard against the AIDS Initiative."

"What the hell does that have to do with it?" Caroline snarls, and takes her money.

By the next weekend Linda's pleas grow more frantic: "My grandmother is dying, I need support."
"There's no one else I can talk to."
"Caroline, please you owe me this one time, let me come and talk it over."

"If you're not back in an hour I'm coming in with the dyke patrol," Pam warns.
"I know I shouldn't, but she's been ringing my phone off the hook, eight times already today."
"So get a phone machine for Pete's sake. Caroline, she'll pull you back in. Don't kid yourself. What about your car?"
Caroline looks away. "I'm going to confront her about the car!"
"Not by yourself."
"I'm not a wimp! I'll be okay."

"Jeez, what happened to the screen door?" Caroline stares at the fist-sized hole piercing the wire mesh.
"Football went through," Linda laughs, catching Caroline's glance. "I was throwing to Shane." Linda shuts the door behind them, and immediately puts her arms around Caroline, squeezing tightly.
Caroline pulls away. "Where's the stuff I left?" She begins taking a house key from the metal ring.
"Let's chat for a minute. I haven't seen you . . . "
"I told you I wasn't coming over for a visit. You said to finish business."
"At least see the garden."
Caroline follows Linda out through the open glass sliding doors. Ferra comes running.
Caroline observes the careful, recent landscaping, hours of work: every bit of nature that could possibly have been considered untidy has been organized,

clipped, and shaped. The roses on the back wall are trimmed down almost to nothing.

"I had to get out my energy somehow."

Linda takes Caroline's arm and leads her to the vegetable patch.

The garden is leafy, crowded, with lush rows of feathery carrot tops, thick onion stalks, tomatoes weighing down their vines, the aroma of basil wafting up through it all. *Impossible that these plants should have grown so much in a week's time*, Caroline thinks.

"I almost pulled the whole thing up," Linda announces.

"What! Why?"

"I couldn't stand to see it. Don't look at me like that, it hurts. It makes me miss you too much."

Caroline's garden suddenly seems a vulnerable little forest. She promised herself she wouldn't fight with Linda, today or ever again. Now she is screaming into Linda's face, choking out: "I am struggling to buy food! People are dying, starving to death, and YOU want to pull up a garden—"

"Vegetables are cheap at the Farmer's Market. Anyhow, it doesn't really fit in with the landscaping."

"I'm going, Linda. Don't call me! Leave me alone."

"Hey, calm down. I didn't pull it up! You say you want me to tell the truth, then when I do, you get pissed at me. I just told you the truth. So which way do you want it?"

"I don't want it at all."

"Let me get your stuff," Linda goes into the house ahead of Caroline; Caroline stands at the door and waits.

"Sit on the couch with me for a minute."

"No."

Linda moves closer, speaks softly: "Please, just a minute, then you can go."

Caroline sits down nervously on the very edge of the couch; Ferra climbs into her lap. She pulls the cat to her chest.

"That cat is driving me nuts." Linda's lips are pressed tight, she holds her hands in fists, low at her side.

"She always drove you nuts." Caroline glances at the door, then quickly back at Linda's eyes. "She's such a beautiful beast."

"She gets into everything, even knocks over Shane's food." Linda moves closer, looks down into Caroline's face.

"Shane loves Ferra." Caroline gulps for air, then keeps talking. "They're good company for each other."

The cat leaps away as Linda moves abruptly, pinning Caroline to the couch. She runs one hand across Caroline's hair for a moment, then kisses her on the mouth, hard.

"I love you. I'll change, I'll go into therapy. I want you. Come back."

"I can't breathe!"

"What if we did therapy?" Linda asks without shifting her position.

"Linda, get off of me. I don't want to go to therapy. We're not together any more. It's dangerous for us to be together."

Linda sits up, furious: "Will you stop calling me dangerous? Telling people that I battered you. You fucking bitch, how dare you?"

"I'm not telling anyone anything." Caroline looks at the door again.

Ferra tries to sit between the women, meowing loudly.

"I'm taking that cat to the pound."

"I'll find a home for her," Caroline pleads.

"If I can't have you, than everything between us is dead. Everything has to die."

"Stop it Linda—"

"No, you stop it, are you coming back or not?"

"I shouldn't have let you go over there!"

Caroline brushes off Pam's hug, exhausted, wild-eyed, in shock. "I want a bath, I want to rinse my mouth. I want to be alone."

"Who is it? Who's out there?" Caroline sits up, fumbling by the bedside for something, some weapon.

The noise comes from outside her window.

Caroline slides the curtain aside a tiny bit.

"Open up." Linda, face barely visible, shouts from the other side of the pane.

"You scared the shit out of me!"

"I need to talk to you," the hoarse voice comes back.

"Go away," Caroline searches with one hand for the phone, for a flashlight.

"Open up. OPEN UP. CAROLINE OPEN UP!" Linda begins to yell and bang at the glass.

"I can't *live* if you don't love me." Linda is weeping into the screen.

"I do love you," Caroline replies, terrified, trying to talk her way out of it. "I love you. If you love me, leave me alone."

Linda is leaning up against the wire, fierce: "No you don't, and I don't love *you*. I hate you! I hate you so much."

"Stop it. I don't care, I still love you," praying the lie will save her, "but you're dangerous to me!"

"Am I dangerous? Huh? Did I bring a gun with me tonight? Am I here to kill you! Huh?"

"I'm calling the cops."

"Yeah, you with all your politics, but when you get freaked out then you want to call the cops, call the cops on your own lover."

"You're not my lover any more."

"Then it's all dead. And I'm going to make sure there's nothing to remind me."

Caroline slams the window shut. She drops the curtain, she lies in bed and shakes. She can't think what to do. She feels that a gunshot might rip through the wall at any moment, or a bottle full of gasoline with a rag fuse explode the sheets into flames. She runs upstairs, and rocks herself in the rocking chair until morning.

Cecropia Moths

I never saw them fly.

In a moment of wonder I saw two moths cradled in the crook of oak branches, shiny rust and wet black, unfolding. Sweaty from the run that brought me there, I stared, thought they might be newly-hatched owls.

My brother and parents knew exactly, swiftly, what to do. They didn't even use a net. Those moths were so fresh, their wings still wet; they couldn't fly.

Ever so gently, the moths were transferred into a shoe box to unfold, monitored so they wouldn't batter their wings in panic or damage themselves attempting escape. As soon as the wings were dry and completely unfurled, each moth was dropped into a Ball jar—a killing jar. A circle of cardboard hid the formaldehyde-soaked shredded rubber at the bottom.

An instant's silent flutter. They died quickly.

Next, each moth was pinned through the center of its fat body to a styrofoam mounting board, a tiny strip of cardboard forcing the wings out flat, fully spread for display.

Preserved, their color and enormous wingspan were a spectacular centerpiece, displayed behind glass. I looked at the box, and at the blue ribbons my brother collected.

Twenty years later that oak tree no longer stands; I don't know where more Cecropias might be found.

I can't bring them back.

Some say I am a woman of secrets, preservation my first impulse.

I still see them cradled, new. I know, now, not to run and shout my joy of discovery. I know, now, to appreciate the honor, to be absolutely still, to tell no one.

Lizards/Los Padres

See I am sitting on a rock overhang. The gorge is deep below. First a shallow running stream, then the deep pools form. Deep pools are below me. Below this rock. Way below. It's not that I'm unafraid to be up here.
Something else. I'm not alone.
On that rock there in the sun, closer to the edge than I dare, is a lizard. That one I call Big One. It is a guard, a statue (almost) in the heat. One more thing, on the next rock (also close to the edge, but not as close as Big One's) is another lizard. Small One.
I remember, I swear: Small One. Yes I do, that is the same lizard that came charging out yesterday—flicking its tongue, flicking: GO AWAY! GO AWAY!
Just a few seconds ago I caught my breath—a big gallump it was, the sudden falling of something from the high cliff into the pools. Up aways from me. Into the gorge.
And both lizards turn toward it. The sound. Instantly. Now; ready to move, up and down, up and down on their lizard legs. Watching: suspicious. Alert. And ready.
And I wonder—should I be too?

I will tell you, this camping area, it is called Los Padres. The name.

Mosquitoes: I said I would take them over the men any day. And this I say knowing the zipper to the tent is broken. So.

Lizards / Los Padres

First thing. They were in groups, several groups throughout the campground. Men. And lots of their beer. And it isn't even so much that I don't drink beer, though it is part of it. It is them and their beer and the music (ALABAMA) and the guns and that they are here at all. So now you know, I draw a hard line.

This is our first camping trip. And we haven't known each other long. And not so well. And we're lovers. That's how it is. We came here because it was an easy drive. Because we don't have many days. Not for the long hike and wooded trail. But for wildflowers and rocks and heat. For me to write.

"Do ya have any mayonnaise?" He's got his hands in his pockets. The guys still in the campsite have turned the music down to hear his appeal to us.
"*No*," she says.
I can't speak. GO AWAY!
"*No*," she tells him and he goes.
"We have nothing for you."

Several six packs they've consumed already and it isn't even dark and the car radio blasts heavy metal and no, we can't hear the birds. Call me a humorless bitch; we moved the tent. Picked it up and carried it across the dirt road. I will tell you, two boys bowling down their He-man dolls with marbles in the dirt by the outhouse were impressed.

The lizards mostly stay perfectly still.

There are Stroh's and Budweiser cans and torn beer cartons on the ledge. Here on the gorge, not far from my feet, from the lizards.

LIZARDS/LOS PADRES

One thing she knows; I grew up in the country.
And I grew up country poor.

You see, I like how alert they become. The lizards. How you might think they are asleep—TAILS RAISED! HEADS UP! Whole body moving up and down, up and down. Tongue out: warning, warning . . . I think I should pack the cans out of here. Away from the lizards and the gorge.

One thing I remember but won't tell her because it is too small; I grew up on a Highway and cars driving past threw their garbage out the window. And I remember my mother picking it up. And how it was to have people throw garbage at you and never even think that you would have to pick it up or live in their trash.

While we're moving our tent the men send an ambassador: "Hey, I hope we didn't scare you away!"
Me, quieter than you might expect but angry: "No you didn't *scare* us." I want to hiss. I want to say: not scared, *tired.*

Still in our new site men are close by, but not as. They are slightly quieter.
One man is chopping at a live tree with a foot-long knife.
"Hey man, this fucking. . .and then he fucking. . . with his fucking. . .so I told him. . .get your fucking. . . and he was so fucking dumb. . . I kicked his fucking. . ."
I crawl into the dome. I don't know her well enough to want her to see that I am shaking with rage. That I may cry. I am trying to think of some joke to make, some excuse.
She comes in and I say, "I try not to hate them. I think that I shouldn't. I just want to be in the woods."
"They make it hard not to," she replies, "hate them."

Lizards / Los Padres

This much my new lover knows: I have eight brothers. I tell her again. I have sisters, too, but that is not what I am thinking about. I have eight brothers, and I grew up in the country and there were guns. And my father.

I know the men must come to the gorge during the day when it is hot. Because of the beer cans. But it is just before sunset and they are down by the river where we first went when I refused to keep going to walk past them even though my new lover said just walk past and I said no and they stared at us like come on and walk by and we are two lesbians and I can't even put my arm around her here in the woods and I said no. *No.*
And that is how we found it. The gorge.

WARNING! WARNING! Small One comes charging across the rock, charging and threatening with its body movement. Miniature Godzilla and its shadow. I can't tell what the lizard knows.

We walk away from the campsite. She likes to listen to birds also.
We walk up the tilted sheet of rock. We open the gate to a meadow, to a path. We climb flats of rock and get cool and silent with the pre-sunset breeze. Many sounds of birds, our heads tilt . . . quick rushing propeller out of the brush: quail. How many colors of wildflowers? Tiny yellow ones make a comforter, soft from the height of rock. Smaller than my fingernail, the purple-centered white ones. The Indian paintbrush. There are craters, gentle, ancient in the side of the flat rock, soft sculptured stone, a large (surprise) cactus, manzanita, coyote droppings, and I think of hawks and rattlesnakes and deer.

LIZARDS/LOS PADRES

We don't see any hawks or rattlesnakes or deer though they would like the meadow below with its stream-fed delicacies along the edge.
It is the guns.

We didn't know they allowed hunting until we got twenty miles in and too far and long to go elsewhere.

Perhaps I will tell my new lover about growing up in a house full of hunters. How they sit at the table and scream at each other and a little girl knows about the whole rack of guns down the stairs in the basement and they shout I'M GONNA KILL YOU and her dreams are of the blood leaking out of her body and the sheriff never comes.
Will she know this: how it tears me, what is my heritage, a love of the country and no country to call my own?

Wear a red bandanna over your brown hair in the woods. How sometimes it echoed. Do you know that sound—only gunfire, never backfire. How it ricochets and you don't go near the woods. What if you live in them? How they called me The Little Girl With the Big Brown Eyes and laughed because I wouldn't come out to look at the deer all strung up from the tree with the gun leaning next to it.

Oh! The little lizard suddenly ran onto Big One's rock. They charge each other—each tail held high in defense. Tails straight as swords.
"This rock is mine. Mine. My space. My rock. My sun." (Big One, or do I only imagine. . .)
Too late. Small One is already past the larger lizard perched on the edge of its rock.
And now they've changed rocks.
And now they've changed places.

Lizards / Los Padres

    Maybe I should have mentioned the third lizard in the first place, but it was so still. The third lizard, the reserved one, had shared the rock with Small One. But now with Big One, because of the switch.
    Big One notices. Body high and rigid: "I know you are there!" Freezes into attention. Watching.

    Maybe we should have known better. We had to pass through an army base to get here.

    Maybe I will tell my lover about the dreams. How I fought sleep as a child. Afraid of falling. Afraid to let go, to be off guard. And then the dreams: of running and being out of breath and hiding in the haybarn or in the weeds on the side of the road and always one of the little ones needing help or giving us away. And the boots coming. And knowing they were near and trying to protect and what to do? Knowing that they were coming for you.
    And waking exhausted. A child.

    Sitting here high on the rock overlooking the meadow; tonight is the full moon. Okay, the gunshot is distant now and their howling faint. The rock holds the heat of the day; a serpent, my body draws it in. My body remembers Diablo and the wide hills and oaks and hiking. That land was not so far from here, though several years ago; it was the heat and land and thinking of deer that made me remember, not the power plant or the National Guard and police and helicopters. It was not being hunted that made me recall.

    I never see them catch or eat anything. All this scrambling for a place on the rock and I wonder if it has anything to do with food at all. Or is it only space.

See, my new lover might say, it was okay; all those guns were for food. For hunting, and you were poor and needed to kill those animals, and don't get me wrong I still eat birds, fish, and yes my family ate those deer and squirrels and rabbits. But listen: they did it for pleasure. You would recognize the look. And how much do you think guns and bullets cost? And it was considered good clean fun. Killing.

Now the big lizard has decided it can't share its new rock any more with Reserved One. I don't know why. It's something to see: a big lizard threatening a medium size one to the very edge of a rock, and the rock hangs over a deep gorge. And will it fall and make no sound, and what if it refuses to go?
But it does. It leaps. Yes, it does, it leaps like I never suspected a lizard could. It leaps to the next rock and doesn't fall between the two into the gorge and it runs fast and lizard-like through the dry dirt and up onto a lichen-covered rock into the shade and poison oak.
And the Big One who has watched begins the ritual once again: Up and Down, Up and Down (WARNING WARNING).

I got mad at her. Just once. Well so what, we'd never fought before and it was the last day and so I walked away, even though I knew I shouldn't I did, because I just wanted to be alone for a few minutes and be angry and write and then come back and it would be okay; so I walked away.
So I walked to the meadow where we went the first night, where it was wildflowers and rocks I could easily scoot up, and I loved going there by myself and was forgetting whatever I was mad about and then I came to the entrance where the gate needed to be unlatched.

The men were sitting on the back of their truck and some were standing and they were right in front of the gate. And they were grinning like they do and looking at

Lizards / Los Padres

me and I felt alone but not alone like I wanted to be. I turned and took a different direction, I didn't go where I wanted to go. I wasn't sure where I was going. I was storming away and they were watching and laughing and I went out of their sight and found a place and avoided the poison oak and just sat and a hummingbird came whirring out of the bush next to me and I got some breath and thought I could write anyway though it wasn't the meadow where I wanted to be.

When we found it, the gorge, we came down the steep path. The first time it was scary. But we were determined. And we got here where it is private and overhung with branches, green. And we got down to the running stream, the place right before it forms into pools.
That is where we soaked our feet.

The men saw where I went. I thought it would be enough that I had gone.
While I wrote not in the meadow where I wanted to be the gunshot came. It was only a few feet away. And again. And loud. I couldn't stay. Not even here. And the only way out was right past the men and they stood with their guns, about eight of them and watched me go. I made myself meet their eyes. I did not look down or away.
But I went.

From up here I can see the water rushing through the gorge, and my lover is just a small turquoise flag midstream.
There is filtered sunlight and fragile shadows. Birds swoop down and I sit very close to the sky.

The lizards: I can't say I figured them out.
Perhaps they do nothing all day but sit on rocks protecting their place in the sun.

Ida	1985
Prom	1986(88)
Sapphire Mountains	1986
Crocks of Kraut	1987(88)
Killing Mice	1986(88)
Marsha: 1962	1986(88)
The Mouse-Gray Suitcase	1986(88)
Glad to Meet You	1986 (88)
The Big Blue Ford	1986
My Mother Played the Accordion	1988
Wishing on White Horses	1986(88)
Cecropia Moths	1988
Lizards/Los Padres	1987

Bettianne Shoney Sien
A too-often tired radical feminist lesbian (with an occasional sense of humor). Born 1957, the eighth of thirteen children. Raised on a small Wisconsin farm. Moved to California in 1981. Never married, gave birth to Isis Amelia Rose Sien in 1982. Shortly after which, Shoney realized that she'd been right at fifteen after all, came to her senses and *came out*.